"Violet, I'm only h...

He was terse, back to holding her at a distance again. "And as much as I'd like to kiss you, and maybe more..." He inhaled sharply. "Given you've never done anything before, I think you deserve to be wined and dined and..."

"Stop being polite." She stared back at him. "If you don't fancy me, just say so. And if there's a Mrs. Sahir at home, or—"

"Violet," he cut in. "I don't like that word."

"What word?"

"'Fancy.' It is..."

"What?"

"Teenage."

"Okay, then." She thought for a moment. "I'll put it more maturely. If you're not attracted to me..."

"I'm intensely attracted to you," he said, and he pulled her in, kissed her neck.

She closed her eyes as lust swept like a turning tide low inside her stomach.

"But I fly back home soon," he went on. "I don't do romance—and, believe me, I *am* a bad choice."

SHE WILL BE QUEEN

CAROL MARINELLI

PRESENTS

Harlequin®
PRESENTS™

Recycling programs for this product may not exist in your area.

ISBN-13: 978-1-335-93934-0

She Will Be Queen

Copyright © 2024 by Carol Marinelli

 Harlequin Enterprises ULC
22 Adelaide St. West, 41st Floor
Toronto, Ontario M5H 4E3, Canada
www.Harlequin.com

Printed in Lithuania

MIX
Paper | Supporting responsible forestry
FSC® C021394

Carol Marinelli recently filled in a form asking for her job title. Thrilled to be able to put down her answer, she put "writer." Then it asked what Carol did for relaxation and she put down the truth—"writing." The third question asked for her hobbies. Well, not wanting to look obsessed, she crossed her fingers and answered "swimming"—but, given that the chlorine in the pool does terrible things to her highlights, I'm sure you can guess the real answer!

Books by Carol Marinelli

Harlequin Presents

Cinderellas of Convenience

The Greek's Cinderella Deal
Forbidden to the Powerful Greek

Scandalous Sicilian Cinderellas

The Sicilian's Defiant Maid
Innocent Until His Forbidden Touch

Heirs to the Romero Empire

His Innocent for One Spanish Night
Midnight Surrender to the Spaniard
Virgin's Stolen Nights with the Boss

Wed into a Billionaire's World

Bride Under Contract

Visit the Author Profile page
at Harlequin.com for more titles.

PROLOGUE

'SLOW DOWN, SAHIR...'

Sahir turned. He'd been a little relieved that the ancient steps carved in the bedrock were so narrow that there could be no conversation, and Mother was some considerable distance behind.

Queen Anousheh of Janana was unsuitably dressed for a rugged walk.

The wind was blowing her black hair into her eyes and her elegant robe was clearly a hindrance. Naturally, his delightfully eccentric mother was in full make-up. Even her footwear was jewelled.

It didn't usually slow her down, though.

Sahir retraced his steps and offered his hand for the steepest incline. 'Why are you wearing palace slippers?'

'They are my walking shoes.' She smiled.

Sahir had not been looking forward to this. It wasn't just that at thirteen he felt a little old for the annual picnic his mother insisted upon. It was more the fact that when they eventually got to the top there was an awkward conversation to be had.

Sahir, much like his younger brother and sister, had grown up vaguely aware that their mother had a *confidant*—whatever that meant.

As heir to the Janana throne, Sahir spent his summers being tutored in protocol and Janana's intricate laws—and a few years ago he had discovered that their mother had a lover!

Sahir had kept that knowledge to himself, but this particular summer their mother's disinhibition had meant his younger siblings had worked things out for themselves.

Something *had* to be said.

'It has to be you,' Ibrahim had said, always happy to avoid a task and volunteering Sahir. 'You're going to be King one day.'

'Mama's going to leave Papa!' Jasmine had sobbed dramatically. 'Oh, poor Papa.'

'She is not going to leave him.' Sahir was firm with his sister. Even if he was cross with Mother, he felt defensive towards her. 'As Queen, she's done nothing wrong—the law states that she can take a confidant—and anyway, Father might have—'

He'd halted abruptly, deciding not to reveal that the King was allowed a *haziyya*, or second wife. Not only would Sahir prefer not to deal with more drama from Jasmine, he could not begin to fathom his austere father invoking such a rule.

'Papa should be kinder.' Ibrahim had been indignant. 'He's miserable and always cross...'

'He has a lot on his mind,' Sahir had reminded him sharply. 'These are troubled times. The King has to focus on peace for our land—not dramas within the palace walls.'

Growing up, they'd all heard their mother taunting the King whenever she felt she was being ignored—telling him that she would take it up with her confidant...saying that at least *he* listened to her, at least *he* noticed what she wore...

It had all come to a head this summer.

Ibrahim had seen her one night, all dressed up in lipstick and jewels, and their mother had urgently warned him not to tell.

And Jasmine, after a bad dream, had tried to get to her mother's bedroom. But the entrance to the *syn* wing had been locked...

'There were no maidens and she took for ever to answer,' Jasmine had sobbed to Sahir. 'Then she wouldn't let me in... just sent me back to bed...'

More worryingly for Sahir, he had seen the sour expression on Aadil's face when a lavish delivery had arrived for the Queen.

Aadil was Sahir's protection officer, but Aadil's father was the King's senior advisor, and if this reached the King's ears there would be trouble.

Sahir knew every rule, and he knew that while a confidant was allowed, all parties *must* be discreet.

Increasingly, Queen Anousheh of Janana was not.

'Oh, Sahir…' Mother was breathless as she reached the top. 'Give me a moment.' She caught her breath as Sahir spread out the rug and blankets he had brought up earlier. 'It looks wonderful.' She smiled. 'Look at all the treats you have brought. It is good for you to learn to do this without servants…'

'I make my own bed at school,' he said, opening the hamper he had carried up the cliff steps and pouring her some iced tea. 'Here.'

'Thank you.' She drank it thirstily. 'What I am saying is that it is good to know these special places.'

Sahir resisted rolling his eyes. Last year they had climbed dusty palace stairwells, the year before they had explored caves… 'The places you take me to are practically inaccessible.'

'Exactly.' Mother smiled. 'So you can do things without others always knowing. You might want a little privacy one day…'

Mother was a fine one to talk about privacy, Sahir thought as they sat drinking iced tea and eating the delicacies Sahir had sourced while they made small talk. Or rather, while Mother attempted to squeeze conversation from her thirteen-year-old son, talking about his life in London and his school subjects, trying to find out about his friends.

'It's a shame Carter didn't come this year.'

'He's spending the summer in Borneo with his grandfather.'

'Poor Carter. To lose all his family like that…' She gave a pensive sigh. 'Does he speak of them?'

'No.' Sahir shook his head. 'He never has.'

Years ago, his friend Carter's mother and baby brother had been killed in a crocodile attack—his father had perished attempting to save them. Sahir only knew what had been said at school or in the press. His friend had never discussed it. Not even once.

'Sometimes it's as if he's forgotten them.'

'He hasn't,' Mother said with certainty. 'Be there for him, Sahir. Always invite him to join us for holidays and celebrations. Speak their names...'

'I've tried.'

'You'll know when the time is right.'

The desert was like an orange fire behind the palace, and the ocean was pounding on the rocks below. Sahir looked to the city skyline beyond.

Janana was a land of contrasts...beautiful and fierce, delicate and wild, mighty yet conversely fragile.

Sahir knew his history, and even if his father was distant and remote he was fiercely proud of him. King Babek of Janana had fought long and hard to have a thriving capital and CBD, with state-of-the-art hospitals, hotels and designer shops, even though the elders and council had been strongly opposed.

For his mother, Queen Anousheh, it was the ancient city and the desert that were her passion.

They both gazed towards the palace, taking in the magnificence of the ancient citadel. From this vantage point the *setarah*—star structure—was evident, but not so the hidden passages and stairs that led to the unroofed centre tower—outwardly bland, glorious within—with its view of the night sky the jewel.

The palace, though a sight to behold, bore the scars of history. Centuries ago an earthquake had devastated Janana, razing buildings, wiping out villages. The fracture had stretched to the palace, where an entire wing had been reduced to rubble, killing the then Queen as well as many palace staff.

Shortly after the earthquake the King had taken his own

life, throwing the beleaguered country into further chaos and turmoil. In consequence the lineage had changed, and so had some of the marital laws. New legislation had been put in place to ensure such a tragedy could never befall the country again. Any future king or queen must have but one passion—the Kingdom of Janana.

Love was for commoners, not their rulers.

'It is such an eyesore,' Mother said, following Sahir's gaze to the destroyed wing.

'It serves as a reminder,' Sahir responded, repeating his teachings. 'A ruler's heart can belong only to his country.'

'Well, once your father brokers peace I am going to fight to have the wing rebuilt and the palace returned to its former glory.'

Mother always had grand plans.

'Sahir,' she ventured, perhaps attempting a gentler approach with her very self-contained son. 'I know that love is forbidden for a monarch, but I do believe that a heart is for sharing.'

'Yes,' he agreed. 'A king's heart is divided equally amongst his subjects.'

'I want you to listen to me.' Mother put down her refreshments to speak. 'Just because you are going to be King, that doesn't mean you have to agree with everything the elders—'

'I don't always agree,' Sahir interrupted.

This topic was one he wrestled with himself. He knew his mother must be lonely, even if she smiled and laughed. And yet he could understand the demands placed upon his father.

'I am learning, and not yet King,' he said. 'Until that time I shall abide by all the teachings.' He turned to face her. 'You do!' At thirteen he had not quite mastered being as aloof as his father. 'Especially the ones that suit you.'

'Pardon?' She blinked.

It had to be said, and it fell to him. 'Your discretion is lacking.'

'Sahir...?' Her head was cocked to the side, her hazel eyes

curious. Perhaps she was unsure about the warning being given. 'What are you saying?'

Sahir held her gaze and refused to blush. Nor did he allow a glimpse of his agony at having this conversation. His voice was deep, that of a man, and he held on to his trust that it would remain steady now.

'There is no place in the palace for an imprudent confidant.'

To his surprise, she laughed. 'Oh, Sahir.' She laughed so much she wiped tears from her eyes. 'You can be so staid at times—just like your father.'

'He is King!'

'Yes…yes.' She took a breath, pressed her lips together and composed her face. 'You are right.'

'Mother, please…' Now his voice croaked…now fear surfaced. Sahir had done his best to reassure Jasmine, but he too was scared of what might happen. 'Be more careful.'

'Sahir…' She held his chin. 'You were right to speak to me. It will be addressed. Now, let's enjoy the rest of our picnic. To-morrow you fly to London, and soon you'll be back at school.'

Sahir nodded, but then frowned. 'Mother?' There was a trickle of blood coming from her nostril. 'You're bleeding.'

'It's the climb,' she said, reaching for a napkin. 'Is there any ice in the hamper?'

'Of course.' He felt dreadful, even if it was quickly sorted. 'I should not have said anything.'

'Sahir,' she reassured him. 'I'm fine.' She put her arm around his tense shoulders, as if she knew how much this conversation had killed him. 'I know it took courage to discuss this with me.'

'You'll be more careful?'

She nodded. 'Everything shall be fine.'

Three weeks later he was summoned from class and told his mother was gravely ill.

Mid-flight home, Sahir was informed that Queen Anousheh was dead.

CHAPTER ONE

'MY DECISION HAS been made.'

Crown Prince Sahir of Janana's deep voice caused a few shoulders to stiffen before his team rapidly stood up to bow. His appearance at the double doors to the dining room was a little unexpected—after all, he was supposed to be upstairs, preparing to attend a wedding.

His Belgravia home was elegant—a white stucco building with a balcony that ran from the lounge to the principal bedroom. To the rear, the gated garden offered secure elevator access to the main residence, and it was large enough to contain flats for staff.

Ultimately, though, when he was in London, it was Sahir's home.

It didn't feel that way this late morning.

His dining room, often used to host small receptions or private dinners, was serving this morning as a meeting room. The silver candelabras had been removed and the gleaming oak covered with a leather protector.

On Sahir's way down from his rooms he had passed palace staff carrying his formal attire for tomorrow up to his dressing room.

Given Sahir's main residence was the palace, he was more than used to staff coming and going there—but in London he had his own staff, as well as a hand-picked team that accompanied him.

The arrival here of the palace entourage felt like an intrusion.

Not only were they several hours early, but Aadil—now the King's chief advisor—had joined them.

Aadil had been a thorn in Sahir's side since childhood. There was a lot of history between the two men—decades worth—and in all that time there were few pleasant memories Sahir could summon.

It had been Aadil who had coldly informed him of the Queen's death.

'Your Highness,' Sahir was greeted now, as he crossed the room and took a seat at the head of the table.

Even caught unawares, with his raven hair wet and his face unshaven, still there was no question that Sahir was the absolute authority as he signalled for them all to be seated before addressing the subject being debated.

'Only minimal security is required today. What else?' He turned to Pria, his private secretary.

'Some minor revisions for tomorrow,' she said, handing him an updated plan. 'It's a tight schedule. We need to leave here ten minutes earlier.'

'I see.'

Sahir flicked through it, his dark eyes missing nothing, noting that other updates had been added beneath the names of certain guests now attending tomorrow's function. Little prompts to aid conversation.

The King and Queen of a neighbouring kingdom had recently become grandparents again—good to know…he would offer congratulations.

Then he saw an added suggestion. Say *Alf mabrook!*

A thousand congratulations.

While a common saying, it seemed a little excessive—especially for the less than effusive Sahir.

He read on.

A sultan's brother-in-law had passed away—he would offer his condolences on behalf of Janana.

But there was another prompt… Say *Atueatif maeak*—I take my sympathy to you.

Just a little more personal—personable, even?

And yet Sahir was neither.

'Sir, should the opportunity present itself…'

Aadil started droning on about some other European royals who would be there tomorrow.

'There was an exquisite gift sent for your birthday—a bejewelled gold amphora,' he went on. 'Perhaps a light reference…?' He turned to Pria. 'Do we have a photo?'

'No need.' Sahir raised his hand to halt Pria from searching through her tablet. 'It will be just a brief greeting.' He looked across the table to Aadil. 'You will have people thinking I'm on something…'

His protection officer Maaz smothered a smile, and even Pria pinched her lips, trying not to giggle. Away from the palace Sahir was a touch lighter, with small flashes of his spirited and wilful mother a little more on display.

'Sir…?' Aadil frowned.

'I thought a member of the Janana royal family must always be composed—not running around shaking hands, gushing…'

'It's a fine line, sir.'

'Not for me.' Sahir was not making light of things now—he could be as rigid and severe as his father. More so, even.

The sudden death of his mother had devastated Sahir, and had served as a rapid lesson in the merits of an icy demeanour and shielding his emotions.

There was a solid black line around his heart.

Impenetrable to all.

Unlike his father, he did not consult aides on his every move, nor meet endlessly with Hakaam, the 'teller' who read the skies.

Sahir relied upon himself.

If he needed wisdom or guidance then he went alone to the

desert—sat with the land rather than searching for answers in long since burnt-out stars.

'Gentle conversation, sir...' Aadil persisted.

'I am not gentle,' Sahir reminded him. 'However, I am a gentleman, and I shall greet all parties respectfully.'

They went through the rest of the plans for tomorrow. He would leave his residence at ten and join the motorcade forty-eight minutes later. He would be back by six p.m., and his flight for Janana would leave at eleven.

'Thank you.'

He went to stand, but Aadil would not leave things there, the question of security clearly still on his mind.

'Your Highness, I must emphasise the high-profile nature of these visitors.'

Sahir felt his jaw grit as Aadil spoke on.

'It would be remiss of us not to increase security.'

'The ceremony today is a private affair,' Sahir responded calmly. 'As for the reception—it's little more than dinner. It's a closed venue, with a select group of guests.'

Carter Bennett, his long-time friend, had in recent weeks married a virtual stranger. The happy couple were now hosting an intimate celebration of the event in London.

However, the post-wedding reception was so low-key that had Sahir not already been in London on royal business he'd have struggled to justify attending. His heavy schedule had for once worked in his favour, though, and he'd agreed to act as Carter's best man. His duties were light. They included attending the cake-cutting at the bride's mother's nursing home, followed by dinner at a nearby restaurant.

The event was so informal he'd been told not even to prepare a speech.

Sahir did not want his presence there to be an issue, and told Aadil the same now. 'Carter has his own security arrangements. Even so, he selected the venue with my requirements in mind.' He turned to Maaz who, along with another officer called Layla, was on his protection team today. 'You're happy with things?' he asked.

It was Layla who nodded. 'The guests have all been vetted. Carter knows not to share your title. The restaurant has been swept and is being watched now, and I'll relieve them as soon as the bridal party arrives. Maaz is about to head to the nursing home.'

'Excellent,' Sahir said. 'As I have already stated—minimal security for today.'

His dark eyes held a strong warning as they met Aadil's, almost daring him to challenge.

'Sir...' Aadil wisely acquiesced.

Sahir dismissed his team...for now.

Most of them were looking forward to an unexpected day off, but a select few remained—and of course Aadil lingered.

Apparently there was one final matter to deal with before Sahir dressed.

Faisal, his major-domo, placed a wedding congratulations card in front of him. Sahir went to take up the jewelled pen he used for royal matters, but then hesitated—after all this was personal.

So little was personal in Sahir's life and so, even though it perhaps mattered not, he requested his preferred ballpoint pen—a twenty-first birthday gift from Carter.

'What is the bride's name?' Sahir asked, pen poised.

'Grace,' Faisal said. 'Although you could just put *To the newlyweds...*'

'Thank you.'

He loathed writing cards, and usually only his signature was required, but given it was Carter...

He wrote some fluff about wishing them every happiness for the future, then scrawled his name, pleased, for once, to leave out his title as Faisal briefed him about the wedding gift that had been selected.

'A two-branch silver and rose gold candelabra from the Setarah collection. The bobèches depict—'

'Thank you,' Sahir interrupted.

He knew the collection. Several pieces were here in London, and while he might have quipped that he hoped the groom would get to keep it in the divorce, the thought wasn't shared.

He made small talk only and never discussed personal matters.

With anyone.

Usually, he loathed giving his heritage away, but Carter, a skilled architect, was working with him on plans for the palace restoration, and would appreciate the treasure more than most.

With the card and gift sorted, he headed to the principal suite.

It was rather like dressing for a full English wedding, Sahir thought as he stood in his dressing room and Faisal handed him his attire.

'Pity,' Sahir commented quietly.

'Sayyid...?' Faisal queried.

'It's a shame that it's just a quiet dinner and a few photos. I actually like a good English wedding.'

'You have been to many,' Faisal agreed.

Faisal helped him into the jacket of his morning suit and arranged the boutonniere on his lapel. An unusual choice, Sahir thought, glancing down at the lilac flower with peacock detail on some petals. To his mind it was rather too large...a touch inelegant, even...

But apparently it was a water hyacinth, and had been flown in from Borneo for the occasion. The bride had insisted, Carter had told him.

Of course she had.

The newly rich were very good when it came to making demands!

Once he was dressed and ready to collect the groom, Layla took Sahir through the final details.

'I'll follow behind. Both Maaz and I shall be outside the nursing home and later the restaurant. If the press arrives, or there are any security issues...'

'There won't be.'

Sahir was confident, but he understood his staff had to be sure and listened as Layla told him the updated security code for the private garden and the exit route at the restaurant.

Sahir memorised it easily, repeating it back as he pocketed the key he would use should the code fail.

His phone buzzed, and he saw that it was Carter calling. 'I'm just on my way,' he told him.

'Change of plan,' Carter informed him. 'We'll meet at the nursing home. Grace wants me to have some time with her mother prior to cutting the cake, to ensure she's calm.'

'Sure.'

'And, Sahir... I know you think this is all about my grand-father's will—'

'Carter,' he cut in, 'it doesn't matter what I think.'

'Look, I know you're not a fan of marriage...'

'Nor were you.'

'Things change, Sahir. People change.'

Sahir had no desire to change, though, and no desire for a cold marriage. And he certainly did not want love. He'd al-ready managed to stall things—there was a private agreement in place with his father that the matter of his marriage would be addressed only when he turned forty.

Although now he was thirty-five, it seemed a little too close.

'You got to choose your bride,' Sahir said to his friend. 'And I am sure you made a wise choice.'

'I have,' Carter said. 'Hey, at least you get to choose your second...'

'True.' Sahir let the small joke pass, even if it irked. His friend knew a little of Janana's royal ways, and he would never understand them. 'Carter, you know I shall always wish you well.'

'I do—but could you also extend that courtesy to Grace?'

'Of course.' Sahir wasn't lying—he hoped that both parties got whatever it was they needed from this union. To him a marriage was as transactional as that. 'I wish you both well.'

'Good.'

'And speeches?' Sahir checked. 'Are you sure you don't want—?'

'It's an informal dinner,' Carter interrupted swiftly. 'No need for speeches.'

'As you wish.'

'I'll meet you at the nursing home. Text me when you arrive.'

'Certainly.'

'Thanks,' Carter added, 'for managing to be here today.'

'Of course,' Sahir said.

'It means a lot.'

Sahir frowned as the call ended. Carter sounded as if this marriage actually *meant* something to him.

But his cynical nature soon returned, and a black smile was on his face as he collected the card and gift Faisal had left out.

Of course this had nothing to do with love.

Driving out of the underground garage in his sleek silver car, he found that he was relieved for some time alone—a rarity for Sahir.

London was looking stunning—and yet he drove away from the gorgeous centre to the outer suburbs, occasionally glancing in the rear-view mirror to see Layla driving the car behind. Maaz, as arranged, was already parked opposite the nursing home.

Sahir pulled into the car park outside a very plain-looking building indeed. Layla followed him, parking a suitable distance away.

He glanced around for Carter, and was about to text that he was there when a taxi pulled up and a pair of black stilettoes peeked out, followed by a lot of purple silk.

Glancing in the rear-view mirror, he saw Layla idly leaning against her vehicle, though he knew she was watching carefully... It irritated Sahir. Why was everyone considered a threat? They would have already vetted the guests—discreet checks would have been made, the guest list gone through with a fine-tooth comb.

He was soon given a swift update by phone, and he glanced at Layla's text.

Bridesmaid. Violet Lewis.

Sahir was sorely tempted to fire back that he'd rather worked that out—he doubted there were many calls for silk ball gowns on a Saturday afternoon around these parts. But, yes, the stunning dress was apt, given her name! The shade was violet, he corrected, not purple.

He thought it a vivid choice when he saw the woman's colouring. Her skin was very pale, especially given it was early September and the end of summer. Her blonde hair was worn up, though there were tendrils blowing in the breeze. She had a purse on her wrist, and from that she took out her phone to pay the driver. She looked happy and carefree, completely unaware that she was being watched by his protection officers. She even laughed at something the driver said.

Sahir watched idly as she retrieved a carefully wrapped silver box with an awful lot of curled ribbons, and then laughed again. He found himself tempted to open the window a touch, mildly curious not so much about what was being said, more to discover the sound of her laughter.

She waved to the driver and then, with that same hand, lifted the hem of her gown and walked in her high heels across the rather dour car park. Her pale shoulders were exposed by the gown, and she moved with flair. She could be walking the red carpet and being photographed, rather than arriving unseen and avoiding potholes.

Sahir remained in his car, in no mood to make small talk

with the bridesmaid, who was now peering through the glass door. Clearly the bride and groom weren't in sight, for she fired off a message on her phone.

But then, as the taxi drove away, her demeanour rapidly changed.

When most women might be checking their appearance in a hand mirror, or perhaps pacing a little, instead those straight shoulders slumped and she leant against the wall and closed her eyes.

Formerly bright and breezy, she now cut a solitary figure in her gorgeous gown. A sad figure, even, because she'd placed a hand on her stomach, as if calming herself, and was muttering like an actress rehearsing her lines, getting ready to step into her role…

Sahir was suddenly on high alert. Possibly his staff were right…perhaps Violet Lewis was in fact a threat…

Though not the usual kind.

Sahir found that he wanted to go over to her and engage in some of that hated small talk.

For he sensed that he was glimpsing the true Violet Lewis.

CHAPTER TWO

VIOLET WAS VERY good at giving herself pep talks.

Oblivious of the luxurious silver car and its driver, she was focussed on psyching herself up for the happy event.

You've got this, she told herself. *Just smile and get through today, for Grace's sake...*

It had been a very tricky week.

She should be used to them by now.

Once a social worker had described Violet's life as a roller-coaster ride.

Violet had begged to differ.

Oh, it was more than a rollercoaster. There were waltz-ers and ghost trains, halls of mirrors... It felt as if she'd been handed life entry to a theme park the moment she'd arrived on planet earth. A social worker had been present in the delivery room, waiting to whisk her away. Then her childhood had been a mixture of chaotic parents interspersed with foster homes.

She'd ached for peace.

For a home...

For a normal family...

Her one glimpse of that had been Grace and her mother, whom Violet had grown up calling Mrs Andrews. Both had been so very kind. There had been cake or a biscuit after school, sometimes help with her homework. At times Mrs Andrews would be putting on some washing and had offered to add her uniform, giving Violet a dressing gown to put on. Sometimes she'd trim her hair. Mrs Andrews had been the one to help with her first period, and had always had plenty to spare when it came to products.

'I bought far too many,' she'd say. Or, 'They were in the sale.'

Josephine Andrews had been more of a mother than her own.

At sixteen, Violet had torn up her theme park ticket.

With the help of a new and wonderful social worker, as well as encouragement from Grace and Mrs Andrews, she had been offered a full time job at the local library and had moved to semi-independent living. She'd had her own room, kitchen and bathroom, and had been responsible for all the bills. Without the chaos of her parents her little home had been tidy, and her bills, even if it had meant living on a lot of soup, had always been paid on time.

She'd soon become fully independent, moving into a flat of her own choice, and though her flatmates had changed over the years—Grace being the latest—she remained there to this day.

Her parents, though they had long since moved away, had left her quite a reputation to contend with.

Now, at twenty-five, Violet was pretty much unbreakable— or at least she appeared that way.

She was cheeky and fun…and everyone thought her a little 'out there'. Thanks to her quick wit and voracious nature, some considered her bold, and even a bit of a flirt.

In truth, it was all a façade. Violet had learnt long ago never to show weakness, let alone fear. Her upbringing meant she was suspicious of men, and had barely been kissed, but lately she was doing her level best to get over all that, and had even joined a dating site.

Her job at the library had always been her saving grace. She loved her work and her colleagues, considered the regular clients her friends, but last Monday her lack of schooling and formal qualifications had finally caught up with her. The powers that be had decided on a restructure, and an HR woman she had never even met had informed Violet she was being given two weeks' notice.

The library was her *place* in the world. As her family structure had changed, as flatmates had come and gone, her workplace had been her constant.

The news, though not entirely unexpected, had shattered her. Not that she'd shown it. But it had shaken her so much that just yesterday she had asked to use a precious week of annual leave before returning to serve out the final week of her notice.

Financially a poor choice, perhaps—after all, she'd soon have plenty of time on her hands.

Emotionally, it had been her only one.

Violet hid when she was hurt, and this had wounded her.

She hadn't told a soul—not even Grace, who was all floaty and insisting this marriage to *the* Carter Bennett had nothing to do with money.

Violet had long been worried that Grace was heading for a financial crisis as she cared for her mother.

She had tapped Carter's name into the library computer the very second she'd heard it, and blushed at the groom's reputation. Then she'd sighed when she'd read about his billion-dollar empire and his wrestling for his grandfather's estate—marriage was the key that would release it.

Oh, Grace...

Still, she thought as she breathed in the late-summer air, it wasn't Grace's choice of husband that was filling her with dread. It was the thought of the little ceremony ahead...

When Violet had been around eighteen, things with Mrs Andrews had changed.

It had started with the occasional offhand comment, which Violet had brushed off. Then a couple of rather spiteful things had been said, which Violet had tried to ignore. It had culminated in a dreadful confrontation, when Mrs Andrews had accused her of stealing a necklace—even threatening to call the police.

That had been awful enough, but it had been the doubt from Grace that had hurt the most and almost cost them their friendship.

But Grace had finally broken down and admitted that her mother had become suspicious and terrified of everyone, and then she had sadly been diagnosed with early onset dementia…

Mrs Andrews hadn't known what she was saying, and Violet accepted that, but her accusation had been so personal, so hurtful, so caustic… Especially from the woman whom she'd adored since she was a little girl.

And the doubt from Grace, no matter how brief, and the glimpse of the knowledge that she might be dropped by her friend had devastated Violet, even if she'd never let it show.

Violet hadn't really seen Mrs Andrews since, but now she was about to.

Mrs Andrews barely recognised even her own daughter, but Grace wanted one happy photo…one shining picture on her wedding day…with those she and her husband were closest to.

Violet felt ill at the thought of it—terrified, not just for herself but of any confrontation that might ruin Grace's special day.

Perhaps she should suggest not going in?

It was something Violet was still pondering as the doors to the nursing home opened. It was the groom—Carter. Violet recognised him not just by the morning suit but by her little snoop on the internet, so she fixed on a dazzling smile and, pulling herself from the wall, greeted the man who was—from all she had read—a completely reprobate groom.

'You must be Carter…' Violet said—and didn't add *the man taking advantage of my friend…*

Instead, determined to get through this day, she smiled and shook his hand.

* * *

Only when Carter had appeared did Sahir get out of the car and approach.

'Sahir.' Carter shook his hand. 'Thank you for being here today.' He introduced the bridesmaid. 'This is Grace's close friend, Violet.'

'Violet.' Sahir nodded, and briefly met eyes that were a vivid blue, though they barely met his. Her interest was clearly fixed on the groom.

With the introductions made, Carter caught sight of the box Violet held. 'We said no gifts!'

'Oh, people always say that…' she dismissed, her voice trailing off as Carter turned and peered through the door of the nursing home.

Sahir watched as, with Carter's back turned, Violet Lewis's smile faded and her blue eyes narrowed in suspicious assessment.

Ah, so she wasn't sure about this union either!

'Here comes Grace,' Carter said, and Sahir watched as the single bridesmaid in this very small celebration turned her smile back on like a light.

'Grace,' Carter said, 'this is Sahir.'

Well, the bride wasn't quite the gold-digger he'd been expecting. She looked sweet and natural.

Sahir was not being cold in his expectations. Not only was he aware of the financial implications of this union, his status meant that at several weddings he'd attended Sahir had been placed in the awkward situation of dealing with a bride determined to flirt—and not with her groom.

Indeed! It was, at times, quite perilous being a prince.

'It's so lovely to meet you, Your… Sahir.' Grace's smile wavered, and he knew Carter would have warned her not to reveal his status. She was clearly unsure how to proceed. 'Carter told me you've worked on a lot of projects together.'

'Indeed…' Sahir nodded.

'We'll only be spending a few moments in there,' Grace explained. 'Mum seems good today, but she can get a little confused.'

'I understand.'

Grace turned her attention to Violet then. 'Oh, you look incredible! Your dress...' Her jubilation faded when she saw the parcel Violet held. 'We said no gifts.'

'You did,' Violet agreed, and Sahir blinked as she went on to elaborate. 'Honestly—it's really the most annoying thing to find on a wedding invitation. As if I wasn't going to buy you a present!'

'We meant it,' Grace said. 'There's nowhere to put it.'

Sahir saw she really was a bundle of nerves as she tried to hand Violet a spray of flowers.

'And you have to hold these...'

'Here,' Sahir offered, and relieved Violet of the box. 'I'll keep it in my car.'

He did so, placing her gift next to his. To his own surprise, curiosity got the better of him and he briefly peeked at the attached tag.

Violet's message was far more effusive than his!

Something about *soulmates...eternal happiness...*

Yet for all Violet's written hopes for them, as he returned to the small party the bridesmaid seemed reluctant to go in.

'Grace,' she said to her friend, 'why don't I just wait out here?'

'But I want you in the photos. The photographer's already inside.'

'I do tend to upset her, though.' Violet lifted her hand in a wavering gesture. 'Perhaps we can just have photos of us outside? Or at the restaurant later?'

'Violet, she won't even recognise you—she barely even knows who I am now.'

Sahir's curiosity was piqued—why wouldn't Violet want to be recognised?

'Ready?' Carter checked, and Grace took a breath and nodded.

It really was a rather odd function…

The couple walked ahead, and as he held the door open Violet stepped in, all smiles as the photographer clicked away.

'Gosh, I thought we'd have a moment to…' Violet muttered, more to herself than him, as they stood outside a lounge room where the small celebration was taking place.

As the bride and groom walked in to the oohs and ahs of the residents he looked away from the happy couple to the bridesmaid.

'Our turn now,' she said, and gave him a smile—no sign now of the nerves that he'd witnessed when she'd been alone outside.

Then he met her eyes…clear, sparkly and that gorgeous shade of blue.

No sign there either.

'Shall we?'

He offered his arm as they were summoned. Moving the bouquet to her other hand, she took it, and he briefly caught her wrist.

There was his sign.

In that second he felt her pulse tripping in panic, felt the ice of her skin. And beneath the perfumed air that surrounded her was the indescribable yet to a trained warrior unmissable scent of fear.

Sahir glanced over. There was nothing in her expression that gave it away. Her hand had positioned itself on his arm, her fingers were as light as a little bird's foot wrapped around a finger, and there was not even a slight tremble that he could detect on the bare arm next to his.

But for whatever reason, Sahir knew she was terrified.

'You'll be fine,' he offered.

'Of course.'

* * *

It was a very sedate affair.

There was a small cake on a silver stand, champagne and sherry had been served, and waiters were poised to serve afternoon tea to the residents.

The bride's mother seemed too young to be in the nursing home. She sat there in a high-backed chair, her hair the same deep brown as her daughter's and her skin smooth, with hardly a line.

'A wedding?' She looked at her daughter. 'Why didn't you tell me? I need to get ready.'

'You are ready,' Grace responded, clearly used to reassuring her. 'In a moment or two we're going to cut the cake.'

'Grace?' she checked. 'You're getting married?' She peered at Carter. 'To him?'

Carter, as if he hadn't been there before, politely shook her hand. 'Mrs Andrews.'

'Violet…' The mother of the bride smiled in delight when she saw her. 'You're here too?'

'Hello, Mrs Andrews.'

She let go of his arm and stepped forward to embrace the seated mother of the bride.

'Josephine,' she corrected. 'I keep telling you to call me that. I haven't been called Mrs Andrews since…'

Then she frowned, and there the pleasantries ended.

'You've got a nerve…' She started to rise from her seat. 'Thief!'

'Please, Mum…' Grace was frantically trying to calm her mother down and throwing anxious, awkward looks towards her bridesmaid, who stood, frozen, as the tirade continued.

'Violet Lewis!' Mrs Andrews sneered. 'The apple doesn't fall far from the tree.'

Only then did Sahir realise that Violet was wearing a dusting of blusher—her face had turned so pale that the pink now seemed gouged into her cheeks. In fact, she looked like a porcelain doll, her eyeshadow, mascara and lipstick painted on to pale, pale features.

Yet still she pushed out a smile. 'I'll go. I'm upsetting you...' Her voice was bright, though a little too high.

Sahir heard the swish of her gown and the click of her heels as she moved quickly out of the room.

'Damn thief!' Mrs Andrews ranted. 'We all know it was you!'

'Mum...' Grace was pleading, but clearly torn, and when Carter stepped in to help, she ran after her friend. 'Violet...'

As he was best man, and very used to taking control, Sahir did his duty and tried to help Carter calm the mother of the bride—but to no avail.

'Who's he?' Mrs Andrews demanded, eyeing him with suspicion. 'What's he doing in my home?'

And Sahir knew it was best that he too leave.

Even though she'd been half expecting it, so many dreadful memories were flooding back, and Violet was deeply shaken as she walked briskly down the corridor.

'Violet, wait!' Grace was clearly distressed as she caught up with her. 'Mum doesn't mean it...'

'I know that. She's confused and doesn't know what she's saying...'

Grace looked as if she was on the verge of breaking down. 'I honestly thought things would be okay...'

'And they shall be,' Violet reassured her. 'So long as she doesn't get another glimpse of me. Go back in and enjoy things. I'll wait outside...' She gave her brightest smile. 'You can make it up to me with champagne later.' Violet squeezed Grace's hands. 'Forget it happened.'

Violet couldn't forget it, though.

She stepped outside and took a huge breath, determined not to cry. Her nails were digging into her palms as she tried to steady her breathing, and she felt a hot tear splash out.

'Damn,' she cursed, thankful that she was alone. Well, apart from a woman leaning on her car—but she was too busy looking at her phone to notice.

Even so, Violet moved to the side of the building.

It was possibly a throwback from her childhood, but Violet loathed the thought of anyone seeing her upset or knowing that she was feeling vulnerable.

Yet despite her efforts to contain them, the tears kept right on coming.

She scrabbled in her purse, even while knowing she hadn't brought a tissue. Violet was simply too used to picking herself up and carrying on rather than caving in to tears.

Just not today.

She sniffed and dabbed under her eyes, then saw the black ink of running mascara on her thumbs.

'Here…'

She started as she saw the best man was offering the pocket square from his morning suit. 'I'd ruin it,' she sniffed. 'You'd never get your deposit back.'

'Take it.'

'Please go.'

'I can't. It's my duty to ensure things go smoothly.'

'So, I'm part of your *duty*?'

'You are,' he said, relieving her of the bouquet.

Having placed it on the ground, he held out the square of silk again, but she didn't notice. Her eyes were closed and she was back to leaning against the wall and scolding herself. 'Stop it, Violet.'

Sahir had another suggestion. 'Breathe.'

She did as he said and inhaled deeply, and then she did it again, before speaking urgently. 'Grace mustn't see how upset I am.'

'I'm sure she doesn't expect smiles after all that.'

'I don't cry…' Violet attempted to explain the anomaly this was. 'I mean, I *never* cry.'

'Violet, you did suggest not going in.'

'I did.'

'Grace should have listened.'

'Yes, but…' It felt important to defend her friend and explain that her tears weren't all Grace's fault. 'It's not just her mother that's upset me…' She gulped. 'It's been a wretched week.'

She took out a mirror from her purse and tried to dab at her black tears, then gave in and asked for the silk square.

It just made things worse, spreading mascara like soot across her pale cheeks.

'Allow me…'

Sahir went back around to the front of the residence and discreetly waved at Layla to stay back.

It didn't feel like enough, though.

Usually he snapped his fingers, or passed problems on to someone else, and he knew Layla was poised to come over.

But he doubted Violet would appreciate an audience.

Taking out his phone, he fired off a quick text to tell Layla it was a private situation, and then stepped into the nursing home for some supplies to deal with a teary bridesmaid.

There wasn't much on hand!

He returned with only a bottle of water.

Violet was hunched over, holding herself, her body a ball of tension as she fought not to cry.

'Stand up,' he said, pouring water on the silk. 'And do as I say.'

'I don't want you to see me,' she admitted, but she did as she was told and unfurled herself.

'Too late,' he said, his voice matter-of-fact. 'Now, drop your shoulders.'

'Why?'

'Because we want you to appear happy and serene for Grace, and we have ten or fifteen minutes to achieve that.'

She sniffed.

'So, drop your shoulders and chin up.'

'Okay…' She forced protesting shoulders down, and when she elongated her neck he saw that it was flushed, as was her chest.

To Sahir's surprise he found he wanted to take her in his arms, to let her cry, but he chose to focus on the task he'd just outlined—to return her to order rather than let her fall further apart.

'I'm truly sorry about this,' she said, and shuddered as he very carefully dabbed her cheeks with the cool silk.

Gosh, her eyes seemed almost familiar, he thought, though he'd never met her before.

'Look up,' he instructed, dabbing gently at the little flecks of black mascara that clung to her fair lashes, and although she did as instructed, she voiced a question.

'How do you know how to do this?'

'I have a very emotional sister.'

Her full, trembling mouth smiled.

Almost.

Then, as he worked on wiping away the streaks on her cheeks, he listened as she tried to explain the anomaly that this was.

'I'm honestly the last person to cry. I mean that. Grace would be so upset if she saw me.'

'Don't think about it now, or you'll get upset again. Think…'

'Happy thoughts?' she scoffed.

'Neutral thoughts,' he corrected, but then he paused, for usually he was not one for admitting that he was anything other than completely together. Nor was he one for sharing the tactics he used when a surge of emotion threatened to hit him, and how he managed to remain impassive even in the most trying of times. 'It works. Just focus on something that you find neither happy nor sad.'

'Such as…?'

'It's different for everyone…something that doesn't excite you.'

'Filing the late returns,' she said. And even though he had no idea what that meant, at least she was talking. 'I don't hate it; I don't enjoy it. I just…' But then she took a shuddering breath and her tears were starting again. 'Oh, I'm going to miss…' She shook her head as if trying to clear it. 'What's your neutral?'

'I have many.'

'Share one.' Her voice sounded urgent. 'Please!'

Those stunning eyes moved to meet his, and while Sahir usually had a plethora of neutral thoughts he could rapidly summon, for a second or two he had none. Her eyes *were* familiar. They were the same deep intense blue of the lapis lazuli embedded in the walls of the observatory. The colour of a clear night sky, with flecks of gold and silver. But they were by far too enchanting to explore.

Instead of dabbing her cheeks, he moved his hand so it rested on the wall by the side of her head as he attempted to find something neutral.

'Cricket,' he said, and saw her nose wrinkle. 'At my school they were very serious about it.'

'Did you play?'

'I had no choice—I was very good at it. I have excellent hand-eye co-ordination. I was captain in my final year.'

'Yet you hate it?'

'No,' he reminded. 'Neutral.'

He knew she smiled—not because of her lips, but because he saw her tears dry and how her eyes shone with the escape he briefly gave her—so he gave her a little more.

'My birthday is in July—the middle of cricket season. I would get tickets to matches, a piece of cricket art, another bat…' He said it with all the lack of enthusiasm those gifts had mustered, and yet he smiled as he shared the memory.

His smile stole her breath—and also the newly found calm he had so recently brought. For how could she summon neutral thoughts as he smiled right into her eyes? How did she attempt neutral when she was suddenly aware of the proximity of his mouth and the fact that his hand rested on the wall behind her head?

He could never know how nervous this moment made her.

Or that she'd never enjoyed male company, even though she'd tried.

How could this man know that she didn't do eye contact when she was staring so readily and so deeply into his eyes?

He was exquisite—but how hadn't she seen it until now? Possibly she'd been far too busy trying to work out the playboy groom to pay attention to his suave, good-looking friend.

On the periphery of her vision she'd noticed the elegant man climbing from a silver car, and as they'd walked to the lounge she had been a little too aware of his exotic scent, but very deliberately she'd paid him little heed.

Another rich playboy, going along with the charade…

Now, though, she met eyes that were as black as night—or were they a very dark navy? She could just make out the iris. His hair wasn't just black, it was raven—a true blue-black, and a shade she'd never seen.

'Breathe,' he told her again, and she was grateful for the reminder—even though it wasn't the prior upset that had caused her body to malfunction again, it was the shock of such beauty close up.

Violet took in his stunning bone structure, his sculpted cheeks and straight nose, then moved her gaze down to lips that were so perfect they had to be the prototype…the one God and the angels had first designed. Every other mortal had got some variation, for these lips she was now staring at were perfection. A little large, but not anything other than deliciously so, and there was a neat pale line around the cupid's bow that made her breath hitch. And how did you get a razor into that cleft in his chin…?

She watched his lips as they spoke. 'Your cheeks are very pink,' he said.

'Yes…' Violet croaked, putting her hands up and feeling their heat as he removed his hand from the wall.

'Can you calm them? So Grace doesn't see you've been crying?'

'Yes, yes…' She went into her bag, pathetically pleased he'd blamed the sudden burning flush on her earlier boo-hoo.

She opened up her compact, but she was all fingers and thumbs. Without a word he took it, but first he offered again the use of the square of silk.

'Blow your nose.'

She did so noisily, frantically trying to think of something to say so that he didn't notice her sudden, almost violent attraction.

It was something she'd never encountered before, and she was flailing as he opened the compact and dabbed powder on her cheeks.

'What's your sister's name?' she asked.

'Jasmine,' he said, as he powdered the tip of her reddened nose. 'She used to cry all the time.'

'And now?'

Sahir said nothing in response.

'Now?'

'Now she's tougher—or perhaps she cries to her husband rather than me.'

He offered the bottle of water for her to gulp and it really helped. Not just with the tears, but to snap her back to her normal senses. Yes, he was being nice, but if he was a good friend of Carter's… Well, according to Violet's research, he must be an utter bastard too.

She must not lose sight of that!

'Why are you looking at me the same way you looked at the groom?'

'What way was that?'

His gorgeous eyes narrowed, imitating hers.

'Birds of a feather…?' Violet said.

'I don't understand.'

'Flock together,' she added, but then felt guilty. After all, the same had long been said about her. Yet she at least had broken the cycle and flown the coop.

'So, you are suspicious of this union?'

'It's not my place to say.'

Even if they both refused to say it outright, it would seem they were both in agreement—this marriage really was a farce.

Still, whether it was his emotional sister, or his hordes of previous women-friends, he knew about repair jobs with make-up, Violet decided as she peered into the mirror.

'Wow, even I'd hardly know. Thank you, Sahid.'

'Sahir,' he corrected.

'Oh, yes…' She took a breath. 'Sahir.' She nodded, as if locking it in as they emerged around the side of the care home. 'And thank you for not asking what that was all about.'

They parted ways as the doors opened and the couple emerged.

'Don't thank me yet,' Sahir murmured, his voice low and for her ears only.

And it might just as well have been dipped in chocolate and slathered in cream, because it was the closest thing to vocal seduction Violet had ever known.

'After all,' he added, 'the night is still young.'

CHAPTER THREE

IF SAHIR HADN'T seen Violet so distraught for himself, he would never have known. She was smiling and throwing confetti, seemingly without a care in the world, as the bride and groom climbed into a waiting vehicle.

'Get in, you two,' they urged.

'I am *not* getting in your wedding car,' Violet said—even if she could see it would house plenty and there was champagne waiting inside. Some traditions stood! 'I'll get a taxi.'

'Violet,' Grace insisted, 'I wouldn't put it past you to get the driver lost.' She looked to Sahir. 'Honestly, she has no sense of direction.'

'I got here, didn't I?' Violet said, taking out her phone to summon a taxi.

But it would seem the best man had things in hand, for he told her to put away her phone.

'I'll take care of your bridesmaid,' Sahir assured Grace.

He already had, Violet thought as she enthusiastically waved them off.

'Wave!' she prompted.

'I am not as good an actor as you,' he said, still convinced this marriage was a farce. 'And aside from that I don't wave…' Sahir paused, then refrained from telling her that his waving was reserved for work. 'Let's go.'

* * *

His car lit up as they approached, and then there was an awkward moment when she had to wait for him to open the door, as she had no idea how to do it herself.

'What happened to door handles?' she asked, sinking into soft leather and trying not to notice the more concentrated version of his scent as the doors closed on them and Sahir drove off. 'And don't you have a passenger mirror?'

It slid down at the push of a button and she rather wished she hadn't asked, as it was rather higher quality than her dusty compact. 'Yikes…'

'You look fine,' he told her. 'You recover quickly!'

'I do.' She topped up her lip-gloss, but then her hand went to her stomach.

'Are you going to cry again?' he asked.

'No, I'm just starving.'

'Do you want to stop for something to eat?'

Violet frowned at the odd offer. 'We're going for a sit-down dinner.'

He glanced at the time. 'There'll be champagne and hors d'oeuvres for the first hour or so.'

'I'll be fine.'

Sahir *felt* her sideways glance, and her shameless curiosity didn't bother him. Really, he was more than used to being stared at.

'Did you get them a gift?' she asked.

'Yes.'

'Even though it said not to on the invitation?'

'I didn't notice.'

He chose not to mention that his staff dealt with all that.

'So, what did you get them?'

He was grateful for Faisal's description of his gift, though he downgraded it a touch. 'A candlestick.'

'Oh, I wish I'd thought of that. I'm usually good at gifts, but I've never struggled so hard.'

Sahir stared ahead; she was good at talking too!

'I wish they'd done a gift registry.'

'They clearly didn't want anything.'

'Well, you got them something.'

'True.' He glanced over, saw her full lips and pointy nose, and thought she was like no one he had ever met. Gorgeous, chatty, teary, funny...

'So, what did you end up getting them?' he asked.

'Guess.'

'I'm not guessing.'

Violet waited for him to do just that, but to no avail. Clearly he didn't wave *or* guess.

'A vase.' She sighed. 'How boring is that? I spent double my usual wedding present budget—triple, actually, given Grace is such a good friend. But I just couldn't come up with anything more exciting.'

He made no comment.

'A tulip vase,' she elaborated. 'I was going to get a rose bowl, but I *do* like tulips. At least while they last...'

Even though he still offered no response, she happily carried on.

'I get them on a Saturday sometimes, after work. But they're generally all collapsed by Monday.'

On and on she chatted.

'Still, they make my Sundays happy.'

They sat for ages at some traffic lights. He could see Layla driving the car behind him, Maaz the one in front, and yet it felt like just the two of them.

Finally Grace paused.

'In Janana,' he said, 'where I am from, tulips were once considered more valuable than gold.'

'No!'

'True.'

'Wow! Well, I'll send Grace and Carter a bunch when they're back from their honeymoon, they'll be searching for a suitable vase, and…bingo!'

'Bingo?' He frowned as the lights changed to green and he pulled off.

'Ta-da!'

His frown remained as he concentrated both on her words and the road.

'They'll remember my gift!' she explained.

'Unless they already have a tulip vase.'

He turned and saw her slight pout. Usually pouts irritated him. Violet did them exceptionally well, though, and she even slumped for effect.

'I'm sure they don't,' he said kindly. Glancing at the time, he saw that it was approaching six. 'We're almost there.'

'I don't mind being late.'

'Well, I do.'

'I bet you're always on time.'

'Of course.' He nodded. 'You?'

'I try to be,' she said. 'But I'm always rushing, and sometimes…'

He glanced over. 'Sometimes?'

Violet didn't answer. She was sure a man as confident and measured as Sahir didn't curl up and hide from the world at times.

'Well,' he said into the silence, 'we're right on time.'

'Yay,' Violet said, but without enthusiasm. And then, still staring ahead, she admitted, 'I'm a bit nervous.'

Usually she'd never reveal such a thing. But, given her performance outside the nursing home, it seemed a little too late to play it cool.

'Why?'

She hesitated, not used to sharing her fears. 'I've never been to a French restaurant—at least not a posh one.'

'It's very relaxed there.'

'I'll hardly know anyone,' she said. 'Well, apart from Grace and a couple of her friends from school, who I never got on with. They're married now. I didn't get an invitation to their wedding.'

'At least you didn't have to come up with a gift for them, then.'

That made her giggle a bit. 'Oh, and her cousin Tanya will be there…even though she's barely been around since Mrs Andrews got ill. She's insisted on bringing her children.'

'I'm used to children at weddings.'

'Well-behaved ones?' she asked, and he nodded. 'Just you wait! Oh, and Tanya doesn't like me either.'

They were pulling up outside the restaurant. It was elegant beyond words; in fact the whole street was just like a postcard. She honestly didn't want to go in, but knew that she had to.

'Even the lampposts are posh.'

'Violet,' he said, and she turned at the calm delivery of her name. 'Why don't we stand close to the kitchen, get some hors d'oeuvres as soon as they come out, and then you can tell me why you are so unpopular?'

'Deal.'

The bride and groom were just getting out of their car under the instructions of their wedding photographer. Violet liked the way Sahir handed over his keys to the doorman and explained their gifts were in the car… He just took care of all the details.

'Our turn,' he said, and they moved in for photos.

She smiled brightly for the camera, seeing that Sahir didn't seem to do much of that either.

He was very…remote.

No.

Polite?

Yes, but that wasn't quite the word...

Formal!

'Let's go in.'

Again he offered his arm, and she liked his formality... how he made walking into somewhere that should be daunting rather easy.

'Allow me,' he said and relieved her of her bouquet.

He placed it on the table with other gifts—clearly most of the guests had disregarded the couple's wishes.

'Now they'll be stuck with a hundred kettles and toasters,' Violet said. 'Serves them right.'

Sahir, while he didn't really understand a world that had kettles and toasters, got the drift.

He liked *her* drift...her constant, ever-changing drift...

And that quietly surprised him.

Sahir was used to chic and sophisticated women. His dates were vetted and they all knew from the outset that their relationship was going nowhere. They were just happy for the elevation his status would bring them, the gifts and the baubles...

Of course Violet wasn't a date, and she endlessly surprised him.

Having escorted her to the back of the room where she was handed a glass of icy champagne, he noticed she shook her head as the trays of hors d'oeuvres started to come out.

'I thought you were starving?' he said.

'I am, but I want something sweet.'

'That's later...' he said, then frowned when the 'starving' Violet politely declined everything.

He had a word with the waiter, and soon she stood there with a plate of cakes and pastries all of her own.

'Thank you!' Violet smiled, biting into a tiny chocolate ice cream cone, smaller than her little finger, and made just for her. 'Gosh, that's better.'

* * *

'You have a sweet tooth?' he said.

'Sweet *teeth*,' she corrected, and then worried she'd misled him. 'Actually, you said it properly. I was making a little joke.'

'I know.'

And suddenly Violet wanted to know more about him. 'Have you and Carter been friends for a long time?'

'Since boarding school,' he said. 'Yes, a long time.'

'You work together now?'

'We have worked together on a couple of projects.'

Sahir didn't really know how to explain them without giving his status away, so he turned the conversation to her.

'What about you and…?' He had to think for a moment. 'Grace.'

'We've been best friends since infant school.'

He frowned.

'Since we were five or six years old. She moved here after her parents broke up.'

'Ah…'

'I guess we grew up together. I spent more time in her house than my own.'

Violet took a breath, thinking back to long-ago days and how lovely Mrs Andrews had always been. How it had felt more like home than her own.

'I shouldn't let it get to me, but I do wonder…'

'Go on…' said Sahir.

'No.' She smiled. 'Best forgotten.'

As Sahir caught up with a couple of people he clearly knew, one of the awful old schoolfriends made a beeline for Violet.

'Violet, it's been ages!' she declared. 'Where are you living now?' Her eyes widened when Violet told her she was still at the same flat. 'Still?'

'Yes.' Violet smiled.

'What about work?'

'The library,' Violet said, not really wanting to add that she'd just been let go.

She kept her smile on as she heard about Mrs Glass Ceiling's stunning career, and then her husband, who'd been a real bully at school, came over. She found out that he'd entered politics.

'He's been nominated to stand…'

'Fabulous,' Violet said, and then stood by as he droned on and on about politics and by-elections and then offered his fake, practised smile.

'So tell me about you, Violet…where are you working now?'

His wife answered for her. 'The library.'

'Still?' he checked. 'You had a Saturday job there when we were at school?'

'Yes,' Violet said, keeping her smile in place.

'So what do you do there now?' he persisted, clearly aghast when she told him she was doing much the same, as if he'd expected her to be running the place by now. 'Don't you get bored?'

'Never.'

She didn't know quite what to say next, but thankfully Sahir came over.

'Violet, we need to take our seats.'

Violet found she was seated at the end of the top table, next to Sahir.

'Phew!' Upset from the small exchange she forced a smile. 'I thought we'd have to be bookends.'

'Were those two your friends from school?'

She nodded.

'They upset you?'

'No,' she lied, but was actually touched he saw through her façade. 'A bit. I'm probably just being overly sensitive.' She gave a tight shrug. 'They were banging on about their wonderful careers.' She knew she wasn't making sense so just said it. 'And I've just lost my job.'

'Okay…'

'Even Grace doesn't know yet.'

'She's not going to find out from me.'

'I just need to get through tonight.'

'And you shall.'

He sounded so sure.

'Thank you,' she said.

'For…?'

'Your help today.'

She was grateful to him for looking out for her. Oh, she knew it was all duty, and that nobody wanted to see the brides-maid falling apart. But it was just nice that he'd noticed the hellish time she was having.

'It'll be Cousin Tanya next…'

'Breathe?' he suggested again, only he said it very kindly. 'We'll talk about it later,' he offered. 'Only if you want to.'

'Thank you.'

'For now, you are going to smile.'

'Yes!'

And she did just that, taking a breath, so grateful to have him in on her secret—or rather secrets. Because he shared her suspicions about the bride and groom too—although admittedly they looked incredibly happy.

It was nice to be here with him. And he was delightful company—taking her through the French menu and managing not to make her feel stupid at the same time.

'I don't want the cold cuts,' she said as she pondered it closely. 'And I am not eating blue cheese. What's bouillabaisse?'

'Fish stew.'

'Oh…'

'You take your food seriously, Violet?'

'I don't think so—I'll eat anything.'

Actually, he wasn't very talkative, she thought, possibly a little aloof and stern, and yet he behaved decorously, his focus on both the people beside him as well as the proceedings—so much so that a woman who must be the wedding organiser came and had a word in his ear.

'Excuse me a moment,' Sahir said.

Violet watched him walk off, stand and speak with the organiser, and as he did Grace leaned over. 'How are things?'

'Wonderful.' Violet smiled. 'Are you enjoying yourself?'

'It's perfect—well, except for what happened earlier...'

'Stop!' Violet warned her. 'It's forgotten.'

Thanks to Sahir, Violet thought. She shuddered to think of the blotchy mess Grace might have come out to see had it not been for him.

'What's Sahir doing?'

'I've no idea.' Violet shrugged, and then as he made his way back to them saw that the wedding gifts were being moved.

'Everything okay?' Grace asked anxiously as he took his seat.

'Of course,' Sahir reassured the bride. 'I've suggested we move the gifts to make room for dancing.'

Content with that, Grace got back to her dream day, but Violet wasn't so easily fobbed off.

'What's happening?' she asked.

'Later,' he said.

She gave a contented smile as she took a sip of her newly poured wine, knowing somehow that he *would* tell her later, and that there were conversations to be had away from the top table.

Then she put down her drink.

'You don't like it?' he checked.

'It's fine.' Violet smiled—after all she was hardly a wine connoisseur.

Sahir must be, though, for he took a sip of his own glass, and realised it wasn't at all to her sweet taste.

And again he was being a gentleman, taking care of her in little ways, for he spoke to the waiter, and soon she was being poured a glass of far sweeter wine.

He noticed her likes.

And when he did speak it was *always* a treat.

'Left and to the rear, wearing floral...' Sahir said as the starter was served.

'What about her?'

'Is that the cousin who doesn't like you?'

'Correct.' Violet smiled. 'Tanya. How did you know? Because she has children with her?'

'Hardly *with* her,' Sahir said.

And she had to smile, because the kids were play-fighting on the small dance floor.

'She keeps looking at you,' he said. 'And I agree...she doesn't look very approving.'

'Hmmm...' Violet said. 'She never liked me—even as a little girl.'

He carried on eating as she explained.

'I think she expected Grace's full attention when she came to visit her.' Tanya really was casting her dirty looks, she saw. 'She probably thinks she should have been asked to be bridesmaid.' She turned her face to his ear. Not to whisper, just speaking in a low voice to one side. 'She thinks I really stole the necklace—the one Mrs Andrews was so upset about.'

'Ah!'

'I'm sure when she tells the story, she conveniently forgets that it was found. Still, as someone said, never let the truth get in the way of...'

She couldn't complete the quote, let alone remember who'd said it. His scent was divine, his ear was as perfect as an ear should be...and, oh, that jaw was so smooth, yet she could see the dark shadow beneath the skin.

Sahir was the most beautiful man she had ever seen, let alone spoken to.

He must have wondered why she'd paused, for he turned his face to her. She saw those dark liquorice eyes, and as their eyes met there was a light tension between them that had her abruptly turning from his gaze.

As the starters were concluded he told her that it wasn't just Grace's cousin looking over.

'There are a few men looking your way…although not with critical eyes.'

'Oh, please…'

'Seriously.' He nodded. 'If you promise you won't turn to look, I shall tell you who your admirers are.'

'Okay.' She needed no excuse to keep staring at him, but was delighted to have one. 'Who?'

'Have you noticed the tall gentleman with blond hair?'

'Really?' Violet gave a delighted smile. 'He's gorgeous!'

'Actually,' Sahir said, 'my description was incorrect—he isn't a gentleman! His wife is at home with their new baby—not that that will stop him.'

'How do you know?'

'He was at my school.'

'Oh…' She glanced down at that delectable mouth and guessed it had been working magic for a very long time. 'And you were an angel, I suppose?'

'Not at all,' he said, almost reluctantly leaning back as her plate was removed. Then they faced each other again. 'But I always made it clear that short term was all I wanted.'

Violet blinked quite slowly, absorbing his words, hearing the subtle warning.

'Your blond admirer makes promises he has no intention of keeping,' said Sahir.

She stared back, wondered what his reaction would be if she told him she was a virgin, and that really she'd barely kissed a guy.

But then she stopped wondering. Because that didn't matter right now. All that mattered was his look, and how she felt that if she were to lean forward now and meet his lips, her mouth would know exactly what to do.

The main courses arrived.

To her relief, rather than fish stew, a rich beef bourguignon was placed in front of her. She glanced down at his plate and saw that he'd been served the same dish—no need to offer to swap!

'I requested the beef for us both,' Sahir said.

'I wouldn't have minded…'

'Violet?' His eyes both smiled and called her a liar. 'You are the fussiest eater I've ever met.'

'I'm honestly not.'

Violet *should* have felt irritated, and yet she was delighted instead.

She'd asked for an extra napkin. And then another. Then given him a glimpse of her lack of cleavage and turned him on as she did so.

'I don't want to spill anything,' she'd explained, tucking herself in.

Sahir found himself ridiculously attracted to Grace's unconventional friend.

'When are the speeches?' she asked now.

'There aren't any.'

'Oh!'

She ate very methodically, he saw, avoiding all the vegetables.

'What about the dancing?'

She loaded her fork and pushed off a pea.

'Do you and I have to…?'

She popped silky mashed potato into her mouth.

'I doubt it,' he said. 'There's no formal order for proceedings—just dinner and a dance if people choose to.'

He watched her chew, even though there was surely no need

to, and was arrogant enough to be certain she was disappointed that they didn't *have* to dance.

God, she was fun to tease—and that was something he so rarely did.

Still, he was oddly put out when, in a lull between the main course and dessert, with the plates all cleared and some couples dancing, she nudged him with a question.

'What about the silver-haired guy? I think he's looking at me.'

Sahir glanced around the room, then saw to whom she referred. 'No. Anyway, he's a bit old,' Sahir pointed out—even though he knew that he and Mr Silver-Hair had been in the same year at school!

'I don't mind that,' Violet said. 'There's something attractive about maturity. I'm sick of guys my age. So...' She met his eyes. 'Is he looking at me?'

'I already told you—no.'

'Really?' She frowned. 'My mistake... He must be making eyes at you.'

As the bride and groom headed to the tiny dance floor, Violet popped a mint in her mouth and proceeded to top up her lip-gloss—no discreet bathroom exit for her.

And now, with her lips so shiny and kissable, Sahir found he wanted a taste of that after-dinner mint more than he had ever wanted anything.

Or rather, he wanted that minty mouth on his...

She stood up and shook off her many napkins—an accidental dance of the seven veils—and he sat there, a little stunned by the impact of her company.

'I'm going to dance,' Violet declared.

He watched her head to the small dance floor...watched as a silver head turned and a blond man moved to stand. And, yes, there was a reason Sahir enjoyed a traditional English wedding...

'Hey,' he called.

* * *

As Sahir caught her wrist, a flutter, a thrill…something that felt like a warm breeze from an open door…brushed through her as he turned her around.

'For the sake of tradition, I believe the best man and brides-maid dance together.'

Oh, they do, Violet thought, smiling because her plan had worked, and this gorgeous, delectable man was hers for the next few minutes.

It was nice to dance with someone so elegant, so beautiful and so magnificently scented.

'What a lucky bridesmaid I am,' she said, breathing him in.

She was bold, a bit cheeky, but it covered up so much shy-ness, so much hurt. But then she winced, wondering if she was being too much. And then he spoke in her ear.

'What a fortunate best man…'

She closed her eyes at his velvet words and fought not to lean on him, just absorbing the moment.

'Your dress is perfect.'

'I know!' She nodded as she leant on him anyway, but then she wanted to share what a find the dress had been and so she pulled her face up to his, and being so close up to those lips and eyes was a reward in itself. 'I only found out about the wedding on Monday.'

'I did too,' he concurred.

'The Saturday before, I was getting my hair cut and some-one was bringing these dresses back.'

'I'm lost…?'

'My hairdresser rents out dresses.'

'Okay…'

'Well, I saw this one and I kept hearing it calling to me as I sat there. Anyway, I ignored it—because I had no reason to hire a ball gown—but then I found out about the wedding. Grace wanted me to go to some designer, but I told her I'd al-ready seen the most perfect dress.'

'So you went back?'

'Yes, only they didn't want to hire it to me because it's booked out for a wedding next week—the bride's actually wearing it. I had to beg, and promise it will be returned by Monday, but for tonight it's all mine.'

'I want to see the back,' he said, and raised her hand.

She actually twirled, and it was fun.

So much so she did it again.

He glimpsed the straight spine, the pale, slender back, and he didn't need a second look to know that she was exquisite...and just breathless enough that, as the music slowed, she returned her head to his chest and leant on him a little more.

He was being incredibly respectful, she thought, even as he held her close. For it felt not quite close enough, and she felt like a mouse who wanted to burrow into him.

She experienced the odd temptation to move in just a fraction, for more of this bliss. And yet, it was a polite dance.

And then she felt the warmth of his palm on her waist, and his cheek next to hers, not quite touching, and she wanted to feel that smoothness in a way that felt new.

'There are so many moving parts to you, Violet...'

Sahir's low voice tickled her ear.

'What do you mean?'

'The missing necklace...the dreadful week...the tears... the smiles...'

Damn, the desserts were coming out. Their dance was over and they were soon back at the table—but now she was itching for more physical contact.

'I chose this for you,' Grace informed Violet, as the most perfect chocolate mousse was served, and Violet gave a smile of delight and sank in her spoon.

'Goodness!' Violet closed her eyes as she tasted it. 'That's incredible.'

Yet despite the deliciousness Violet didn't quite finish it, because the dancing had started up again and she was back in Sahir's arms, resting her head on his chest. She reminded herself that she was terrified to kiss—dreadful at it—and yet she had never, ever wanted to kiss someone so badly.

It was all part of a bigger problem. Her childhood had been confronting at times. The company her family had kept had ensured she put a chair to her door at night, and not every foster home had been perfect.

Violet had quickly worked out that showing fear made her vulnerable, and had adopted a chatty, breezy persona. Her teenage years had been even worse. Visiting her father in prison, she had experienced comments and looks from some of the men there. Instead of quivering, she'd spoken up and out, even when she was scared on the inside.

Now, at twenty-five, she wanted to trust…wanted what came so naturally to others to unfold for her.

Yet any hand closing around hers felt like a vice, and any mouth on her own caused a dreadful panic, even though she fought it, persisted, hoping that in the end it would fade.

Why, when she ached for affection, didn't she want to kiss anyone?

Or have sex?

She didn't even like touch…

Only, Violet amended, it would seem that suddenly she did.

Sahir's touch.

The sense of unease she seemed to have lived with for ever had dimmed. In fact, it had dispersed completely—only noticeable by its absence. For in his arms, with the brush of his cheek against hers as he moved closer to speak, she imagined his lips finding hers…

Sahir's low voice didn't jolt her—it felt like a caress. At least until her dizzy mind deciphered his words.

'The music has stopped.'

Violet blinked, as if snapped from a trance. 'So it has...'
She pulled back from his embrace, a little flustered as to
where her mind had just been, for it felt as if they'd kissed.
'I was miles away.'

'And me.'

CHAPTER FOUR

'I BELIEVE THE cake is coming out.'

Sahir unravelled her reluctant arms and peeled her body from his.

'They've already had a cake,' Violet grumbled—but only because she'd far rather dance. 'And I don't really...' She halted, deciding not to mention that she didn't like fruit cake.

Perhaps she was a fussy eater after all, Violet pondered, retaking her seat at the top table. Only Sahir didn't join her. Instead he stood by the dance floor, speaking with the bride and groom.

'They lied,' Sahir said when he came back.

'About what?'

'There will be speeches after all.'

'Oh,' Violet said.

'Slightly irregular order, though,' he said. 'If the cake is to be cut now.'

'Irregular?' Violet frowned.

'Usually the cake is cut at the end.'

'Only if you're a stickler for protocol.'

'I am.'

She didn't envy Sahir having to make this particular speech. The bride's parents were both absent, the groom's family all dead.

She swallowed. 'Are you going to mention his family?'

Sahir didn't respond, and she wondered if he was pondering the same.

The cake was being cut, and as coffee was served, slices came round...

Fruit cake.

Violet chopped it up, to look as if she was eating it, nibbling on the white icing and hoping the speeches were short as she wanted so badly to dance again.

There was no father of the bride, so the groom spoke first, thanking his bride, the bridesmaid, and also the guests.

'Sorry to tear you away from an excellent cricket match...'

A few of the guests groaned, and then Carter glanced over to his best man.

'Sahir, I'm sure you weren't best pleased when I told you the wedding was today.'

Sahir spread his palms, as if admitting it had been a difficult choice he'd been forced to make to attend the wedding and not the match.

She was the only one here who knew his true feelings on cricket, Violet realised. And it *thrilled* her to share in a tiny secret. So much so that beneath the table she pressed her knee against his leg and he pressed back.

She wasn't flirting, and nor was he—it was just a moment shared, Violet thought as the groom moved his speech on.

'I've attended several weddings, where—as many of you have reminded me—I've repeatedly stated that you'll never be getting an invitation to mine.' His voice moved from light-hearted to reflective. 'But then I met Grace, and everything changed...'

'Please...' Violet muttered, but for Sahir's ears only.

'Violet,' Sahir warned. 'He's about to toast you.'

Whew! Just in time she pushed out a smile as everyone raised their glasses.

'To the bridesmaid!'

Then, with Carter's speech over, it was time for some slushy

words from Grace. Violet felt anxious as she watched her friend
give her heart to him in front of everyone. So much so that as
the speech drew to a close she found she was twisting the white
napkin in her hand.

'Carter,' Grace said to her husband, 'I'm so excited to take
this journey with you.'

Violet could hear the adoration in Grace's voice and it worried her—because Grace seemed to be entering this marriage
with a heart brimming with hope. Yes, Grace was strong—
after all, she'd been through a lot with her mother—but life
had taught Violet to be tough, to *expect* to be let down, and
she was terrified that her friend was about to be.

But then she felt Sahir's hand come over her own, in a gentle prompt that she was letting her suspicions show, and she
put down the napkin.

'You seem to think he's playing her,' Sahir whispered, making the hairs in her ears tickle. 'Have you considered it might
be the other way around?'

'Not for a second.'

'Perhaps they are both happy with their choice?'

'I hope so.' Violet nodded. 'I really do. And if that is the
case…' She met his eyes. 'Perhaps you ought to mention…' She
swallowed, loath to give this suave man any advice.

As if he'd take it!

As Sahir stood and took the microphone a deep hush de-
scended. The guests had been still and quiet for the bride and
groom, but there was something about Sahir that had the waiters stopping, the bar staff too. He commanded the room.

'Good evening,' he stated, and looked to the intimate gathering. 'Most of you I already know, or we've been introduced
tonight, but for those I haven't met I am Sahir, a long-time
friend of the groom.'

He got the formalities out of the way—complimenting the
bride, accepting the toast to the bridesmaid, and Violet duly
raised her glass. She was curious to hear him speak. He told

the guests how he and Carter had shared a dormitory at boarding school. How some summers Carter had joined his family in Janana.

He said nothing to embarrass the groom or his bride. It was rather formal and really a very polished speech. Still, Sahir's voice made her toes curl. It was heaven to have an excuse to look at him properly, even if she could only really see his back as he turned to address the bride and groom.

His suit was perfection. It skimmed his broad shoulders and contoured his torso and moved as he spoke. His hair too was immaculate, cut into the nape of his long neck…

Then she heard a slight shift to his tone.

'Before we came to the restaurant this evening I had the pleasure of meeting Mrs Josephine Andrews—Grace's mother.' He looked directly at Grace. 'It was wonderful that she could share in this day.'

Violet watched as Grace pressed her lips together and nodded, clearly moved that her mother had been properly named and mentioned.

'And, Carter…'

Violet found she was holding her breath.

'I never met your parents, but from all I have heard about them Sophie and Gordon would have been thrilled to be here today.' He looked right at Carter. 'I am your oldest friend, and I'm proud to be your best man, although I wish—as you must— that this speech was being delivered by Hugo.'

Violet watched as Carter briefly looked down and reached for Grace's hand, before everyone raised a glass to the people missing tonight.

It was the first time Violet had truly considered that this love might be real.

Just as that thought formed, Sahir moved his speech to a close, ending it on an upbeat note. 'I believed Carter when he said he'd never marry.' There was laughter all round. 'It is good to prove him a liar...' He raised a glass. 'To Grace and Carter—we all wish you every happiness.'

As everyone took a sip of champagne Sahir sat down. Unlike every other mortal, he didn't ask her if that had been okay, or if he'd said too much.

Violet turned to him. 'I think I'm going to cry.'

'Not yet...' He turned and gave her a slightly bemused smile. 'It's your turn to speak.'

'No!' She shook her head. 'I don't do speeches.'

'Violet...' Grace whispered loudly, urging her to stand.

'I can't,' Violet protested. 'I've never...'

'You'll be wonderful.' Beneath the table, Sahir gave her thigh a tiny squeeze. 'It's all very low-key...just keep it short.'

Violet stood on shaky legs and wished she could be as effortless and polished as Sahir.

She had never given a speech—well, just once, for Mrs Hunt at the library, when she turned sixty.

And she'd stuffed that up.

Then she saw her beaming friend, thought of her gorgeous dress, and knew she was the most polished she was ever likely to be. As well as that, she could feel the little aftermath of that touch on her thigh and it was a nice distraction.

'This is all so unexpected,' she began. 'The wedding...giving a speech...'

Violet smiled brightly at the select invitees, and then looked at the glaze on Grace's eyes. Even if she wasn't certain about this marriage, perhaps being happy for a little while was enough...

'I was hoping Grace would bring me back a nice surprise from her trip to Borneo,' she told the audience. 'A toy orangutan, or even a tea set...' She heard laughter. 'And I did get a surprise—just not quite what I had in mind. I suspect she and Carter have been a little too busy to shop.' Violet smiled at her friend. 'So I'll have to wait for something gorgeous after the honeymoon.'

She picked up her glass and toasted the seemingly happy couple.

'To Grace and Carter—you owe me a present.'

She sat down to happy applause, and of course worried that she'd got it all wrong.

'Well done,' Sahir said.

But suddenly there was no time to discuss speeches, or anything. She saw Sahir glance down at his jacket and heard the buzz of his phone.

'I'm just heading out for a moment,' he told her.

'Sure.'

Sob!

She politely shook her head at Mr Blond when he approached, and said her feet were killing her, and then for a moment she sat alone.

She looked at Grace, her eyes closed as she danced with her husband, and then she looked at the groom and how tenderly he held his bride.

Was it love?

After all, who was she to judge when love was something she'd never really known?

Could it be that Grace and Carter were for real?

'You've got a nerve.'

Violet turned to see a derisive look from Tanya. She hadn't seen her since *'the incident'*.

'You might have managed to convince Grace,' she went on. 'But we all know you took advantage of Aunty Jo.'

'Tanya…' Violet took a breath, upset that Tanya still held such resentment. 'It's Grace's wedding—'

'And there you sit, as if butter wouldn't melt in your mouth.'

It dawned on Violet that Tanya's resentment was probably because neither she nor her children were at the top table. 'I honestly think—'

'There's nothing *honest* about you, Violet.'

She breathed in sharply, both at the accusation and also at the sudden sound of Sahir's voice.

'No need for introductions! You must be Tanya.' He was being utterly charming, and clearly hadn't a clue what had just been said. 'I've heard so much about you.'

'Oh!' Tanya positively glowed. 'Yes, I'm Grace's cousin.'

She turned on her charm for Sahir, and as they stood chatting Violet left them to it and took a seat back at the table. She felt silly all of a sudden, wondering if she'd misread the closeness they had shared. Was he simply suave and delicious with everyone?

The night was winding down, and she rummaged in her bag for her phone, to call a taxi.

Two accusations in one day were just too much, and Grace would barely notice if she was gone… She just wanted to slip away.

'Hey.' Sahir was beside her. 'Where are you going?'

'I think I've had enough.'

'We're supposed to wave them off.'

'You don't wave,' she reminded him, but then her shoulders slumped. Of course she had to stay to the end. 'I'll head off after the happy couple leave.'

'Do you need a break?'

Violet nodded. 'I might just nip to the ladies'.' Though knowing her luck another blast from her past would be in there. 'Or just sit somewhere else.'

'I have a key.' He showed it to her.

'To where?'

'There's a courtyard near the main kitchen.'

She frowned. 'Why would you have a key to that?'

'In case there's an issue.'

'Or in case you want to go for a snog?'

She made him laugh. She was direct, and funny, but also, he understood, suddenly wounded and sad.

'No, it's because…' God, he did not want to explain the complexities of his life—he wanted to escape them. But thankfully Violet came up with her own reason.

'Because you're the best man?'

'Yes!' He nodded, content with that explanation. 'I asked for the gifts to be locked up out there.' He told her a part of the truth. 'Cousin Tanya's children were trying to open them. Take it…go and have a little break. You've done incredibly well.'

'Honestly?'

'Here.' He handed her the key. 'Take your time.'

'I don't know…'

'Do you want me to come?' he offered, and before she could give any response, spoke on. 'For that talk?'

'What talk?'

'The one I said would have to wait.'

Violet thought for a moment. Yes, she had hoped to talk to him later. She'd been looking forward to it, in fact.

This time with Sahir had been wonderful—it was others who had soured the night. And so she nodded.

'I'd like that.'

'And me.' He glanced to the happy couple, who were draped around each other. 'I doubt they'll miss us.'

He took a bottle of champagne and she discreetly followed him, but it was all a bit of a maze.

Some events you didn't want to attend turned out to be the most surprising of pleasures, she thought, as she unlocked a door and found a courtyard lit with fairy lights. It was the size of a small bedroom, really, but it felt like a magic garden…

'Oh, my…' Violet breathed and handed him the key, sighing in relief as he locked them in the courtyard and the wedding inside faded. 'I can stop smiling now.'

'Yes,' Sahir said. 'It's just us.'

She just closed her eyes and stopped smiling, and it was possibly as nice as taking her heels off would be later.

'Tell me about this dreadful week,' he said.

'I don't want to bore you.'

'If you do, I shall put up a hand for you to stop.'

She giggled. He made it so easy to just be herself.

She took a seat on a small stone bench. 'Your speech was lovely.'

'Stop trying to change the subject. I want to hear about you. You said you lost your job?'

'I found out I was being let go about ten minutes after I found out about the wedding. Well, they've offered me a part time role at a library on the other side of London, but it's less money and it would mean moving.' She sighed despondently. 'Usually I'd discuss it with Grace, but…' She put her hand up, gestured to the laughter and music. 'I didn't want to bring the mood down.'

'Talk to me, if you like.'

Violet thought for a moment. It had been so hard not talking about it.

'I don't want to leave,' she stated. 'I've been there for more than ten years.'

'You look too young to have worked anywhere for ten years.'

'I started there when I was fourteen, just on a Saturday, then I did a couple of evenings a week, then worked full time when I was sixteen.'

She took his rather messed-up silk pocket square out of her purse and blew her nose.

He was thankfully silent, and he stood rather than sat, but not in an overbearing way…more in a way that gave her space as she sat and pondered her life.

She looked around the pretty garden, its walls dulling the sounds of laughter. It was a relief to escape, and even better not to be hiding from the world alone.

'Do you want a drink?' he offered.

She nodded, and he popped the cork and handed her a glass of champagne.

'Cheers.'

'To what?' Violet asked, but she did clink his glass. 'I've got no job, no qualifications, and my flatmate has just gone and got married...'

'You mean Grace?'

Violet nodded. 'The flatmate I had before Grace used to cook fish for breakfast...the one before that had this awful boyfriend... There's quite a list.'

'Do you have to share your flat?' He winced. 'Sorry, that's thoughtless.'

'Believe me, it's the same question I'm asking myself. But, yes...' She took a sip of icy champagne. 'There aren't many jobs near me, though. Well, not that I've seen.'

'Could you take the part-time job for now? Move closer...?'

'I don't want to move.'

'Because you don't want to be away from your family?'

'No.' For the first time she gave a frustrated shake of her head. 'Nothing like that.'

Violet had been open with him—more open than with anyone—but she chose not to answer that one. She just gave him a shrug, brushed the question off.

'It's just been a bad week.' She rolled her eyes. 'Oh, and I had a dreadful date on Saturday, just to kick things off...'

'Haircut day?'

'That's the one.' She smiled, appreciative that he'd been listening. 'He seemed nice, but when we met he was all about himself—how he went to the gym, how he took care of his body... Do you know? I felt judged when I ordered dessert!'

'In my country you are judged if you *don't* eat dessert.'

Violet smiled for the first time since entering the garden, and for Sahir there was a surge of triumph at watching her lighten, seeing the return of her gorgeous smile.

He gave a shake of his head, as if to clear it. He'd been right when he'd said there were a lot of moving parts to Violet—a lot of life, a lot of personality, and dots he would rather like to join up.

'Had you been dating long?' he asked, disliking no-dessert guy immensely—or rather, the thoughts he conjured.

'No. Just chatting online.'

'Online?'

'Yes. He described himself as "laid-back and easy-going".'

'Doesn't that mean you'd have to do all the arranging and he'd have no problem with you getting the bill?' Her little laugh made him smile and he was curious. 'So, how would you describe yourself?'

'Laid-back, easy-going...'

'Violet!' He chided her for her fib, calling her out, and was gifted another smile.

'I don't really,' she admitted. 'My bio describes me as "outgoing and friendly", and I guess I am. I just...'

She was more than that, he thought, but she didn't know how to reveal her fears and wants or insecurities.

'I'd be dreadful online,' Sahir admitted, and watched her put her elbows on her knees and look up as he spoke. 'I'd have skipped straight past the "outgoing and friendly" Violet, and look at what I'd have missed...'

'That's nice of you to say.' She smiled again as she gazed up at him. 'It's hard out there—not that you'd know. I can't imagine you'd have to resort to going online.'

Sahir said nothing at first, just looked at her sitting there, a little pensive and doleful, yet still but a second away from a smile. That much he knew about Violet. A thought came then—one he'd never so much as briefly entertained before. He had wealth, stature and dates aplenty, but when it came to the future Violet Lewis had something he'd never know—choices.

She also had the prospect of love.

It wasn't something he wanted.

Sahir had grown up knowing he could never be too close to another person, and that it was forbidden to love your wife. After the death of his mother, he had better understood the reason for that law—for how did you run a country on the edge of war, as his had been then, while dealing with the loss of the love of your life?

Certainly he did not want a confidant or a second wife. One would be enough to deal with, let alone two!

Sahir had asked that the subject of his marriage not be discussed until he neared forty. The King was growing impatient, though. The elders too… He doubted it would be put off until then.

No, he would not be going online. His bride would be selected for him, with the welfare of both their countries in mind. It was the one area in his life where he had no say in the matter.

Sahir answered her at last. 'We all have our own mountain to climb.'

'We do,' she agreed. 'Thanks for being there for me today. You've made things a whole lot better.'

'So have you.'

'I mean it,' Violet said.

She sat up, taking in a breath.

Yes, Sahir thought, she'd faced a few demons today.

'Don't worry about Mrs…'

He paused. Usually he was brilliant at summoning names—half his life was spent doing just that, and talking with people he barely knew—and yet since Violet had stepped out of that taxi minor details were proving a little difficult to recall.

'Andrews?' she finished for him.

'Yes.'

'And thank you for saving me from my brilliantly successful, very happily married schoolfriends.'

'If it's any consolation, the two of them were having a big argument outside when I was on my phone,' Sahir told her. 'And as for people like Tanya…'

'I thought you two were getting on?'

'No, I was trying to divert her from being so awful to you. My mother used to say that a snake waits in the shadows to strike.'

'Used to?'

He nodded, but said no more on the subject than that. 'I saw Tanya make a beeline for you the moment you were alone,' he told her.

'Is that why you came over?' she asked.

'Of course. I knew she was going to attack.'

'But you were so nice to her.'

'No. I was *polite* to Tanya. With you, I'm nice...' He offered his hand. 'One more dance?'

'Can't we stay out here a little longer?'

'I meant, let's dance here...'

It was a lovely slow dance, but he could feel her question coming—her need for more information.

'Your mother used to...?' she checked.

'She died when I was thirteen,' Sahir said. 'It was...' He took a breath. 'I was told it was sudden.'

'Told?'

'I'm not so sure. I wish I had acted sooner,' he admitted. 'Noticed things.'

Sahir had told her only a little, yet it was by far more than he had ever told anyone.

He looked down at her. 'Do you find that people talk to you, Violet?'

'All the time. Clients at work, people on buses... I'm the one they sit next to...'

'Taxi drivers?' he added.

'Oh, yes.' She smiled, and her eyes were misty, her next words soft. 'Not so much you, though.'

'You have no idea...' Sahir said.

He was beyond private—no one knew his thoughts—and he tried to pull back control, lighten the topic.

'Let's work on your online bio. How about "gorgeous"?' he started.

But the thought of helping her meet another man didn't lift his mood, so instead he gave up on conversation and lightly kissed her pale shoulder. Then he opened his mouth. As his tongue met her flesh she exhaled sharply, and he lifted his head as she jolted.

'Okay?' he checked, a little bemused by her reaction, and was pleased to find she was smiling.

'Don't stop,' she told him.

So he got back to the shoulder he'd made wet.

'I actually got a shiver down my spine,' she told him. 'I never really got what that meant before.'

'Good,' he said, and his lips moved along her collarbone to her neck, then up to her gorgeous mouth.

Violet stopped him, as if she had something she thought she really ought to say. 'If I'm honest, I think you'd skip past my bio.'

'How come?'

'Because I've never…*been* with anyone.'

'Sorry?'

'I've barely kissed, let alone slept with anyone.'

Sahir met her eyes. Yes, there were so many parts to Violet—but he had a rather urgent question.

'You didn't put that on your bio?'

'Of course not!'

'Because you'd get every—' He stopped himself.

'I do know!' she shrilled, all indignant.

And then he saw her pink cheeks, and she hid her head in his chest as they continued their dance.

'Dreadful, isn't it?' She sighed.

'Of course not,' he said.

'Then why are you holding me like it's a duty dance now?'

'I'm not,' he refuted, even though she'd made a very good point.

'If my date hadn't been so mean…'

'Can we stop talking about him?' Sahir snapped, appalled at the thought of Violet with him. With anyone. 'Were you going to sleep with him? Someone you'd just met online?'

'I wanted it out of the way.'

'It's not a chore! It can actually be...' He halted, perhaps for his sanity's sake. 'Well, you'll find out for yourself,' Sahir said, and then a little too hastily added, 'Someday.'

Only that little addition didn't help his sanity either. He didn't want to entertain even the thought of her with another man—certainly not while holding her in his arms.

Violet wanted to find out.

And not just someday.

Today—or rather tonight.

With Sahir.

She wasn't surprised at the sudden strain between them.

She was good at a little flirting, even if it was usually an act. Yet with Sahir it had been so natural.

'I had a pretty wild family,' she told him.

It was too much, and too hard to explain, but they were dancing more easily now, and he smelt so divine, and *gosh*, he was good to talk to—or was it that he simply didn't say that much?

She was brave enough to lift her head and look at him now. 'And in trying not to emulate them I think I went too far the other way. Became too cautious...'

'Go on...' he invited.

'Now, when a guy finds out I've never slept with anyone, they seem to assume I'm saving myself for a reason. That I want a husband.'

'You don't want to marry?'

'Absolutely I do.' Violet nodded. 'Not yet, though. I want a gorgeous life, with babies and...' She gave a contented sigh, thinking of everything she'd never had. 'But before all that I want to sort myself out. Maybe when I'm about thirty...'

'That's the age you'll be all sorted?' He smiled.

'I hope so.' She nodded. 'How old are you?'

'I just turned thirty-five, and believe me…'

Sahir paused, reminding himself that his future was more than sorted. It just didn't feel that way right now.

Thankfully she didn't notice his silence, just chatted on.

'For now, though, I just want to date…have some fun while I work things out. The trouble is, I don't think I've ever really wanted to…'

That pulled him out of his own head. 'Have sex?' he asked.

'Oh, it's far worse than that,' she admitted. 'I don't even really like kissing. I've never wanted to…never felt compelled…'

Violet chewed her lip, because she'd been utterly honest with Sahir so far.

However, as of now, she was lying.

'Never?' he checked, his hands hovering near her torso and warm on her waist.

'Maybe a little once…'

'Possibly tonight?'

'How did you know?' She laughed.

'I think we were kissing on the dance floor,' Sahir told her. 'Not physically, but… I don't know the word in English. *Takha-tari*…in our minds…'

'Imagining?' she asked.

'Both imagining,' he said. 'At the same time.'

'Ooh, *takhatari* kisses. I like that.' Whatever it meant. 'And you're right—I was thinking about you, about kissing you, maybe…'

She watched his dark eyes looking up somewhere to the left, as if he was really thinking about things, and then they came back to her, and for the first time she saw their colour, the tint on the edge of his pupils as raven as his hair.

'You want to "get it out of the way"?' he accused, using her own words.

'No.' She shook her head. 'It doesn't feel like that with you.'

'Violet, I'm only here for tonight.' He was terse, back to holding her at a distance again. 'And as much as I'd like to kiss you, and maybe more…' He inhaled sharply. 'Given you've never done anything before, I think you deserve to be wined and dined and…'

'Stop being polite.' She stared back at him. 'If you don't fancy me, just say so. And if there's a Mrs Sahir at home, or—'

'Violet,' he cut in. 'I don't like that word.'

'What word?'

'"Fancy". It is…'

'What?'

'Teenage.'

'Okay, then.' She thought for a moment. 'I'll put it more maturely. If you're not attracted to me…'

'I'm intensely attracted to you,' he said, and he pulled her in, kissed her neck.

She closed her eyes as lust swept like a turning tide low inside her stomach.

'But I fly back home soon,' he went on. 'I don't do romance—and, believe me, I *am* a bad choice.'

'I think you're the perfect choice.'

'How so?'

She smiled. 'Because I'm twenty-five and I have never even come close to being so intensely attracted to anyone. And I don't care if I never see you again…' She looked into his eyes and ran a hand through his raven hair. 'Well, I care. But I think you'll be rather deliciously missed and very fondly remembered.'

'Violet,' he said. 'That's a really bad reason to sleep with someone.'

'Oh, so you only sleep with someone when you have excellent, well-thought-out reasons? Tell me, Sahir, what are they?'

'I can tell you why we shouldn't,' he volunteered. 'I don't bed virgins.'

'*"Bed"* virgins!' She laughed. 'Gosh, that's old-fashioned. Well, then, for tonight I shall remain un-kissed and un-bedded.'

She knew she'd hit every nerve, and it had him pulling her right in. She slipped her hands beneath his jacket.

'You are…' He stopped, as if trying to find a word to describe her. 'Irresistible.'

'So are you.' Violet nodded. 'And you have no idea how long I've waited to feel like this.'

'Like what?'

'Ready.'

She wasn't begging, she was tempting him. And her mouth was right by his, and she was completely free to be herself, to cajole and tease. Because he made it so…

His shirt was crisp beneath her palms and she thought of the skin beneath, and of tasting his breath while locked with his eyes. And whatever *takhatari* kisses were, they must be sharing them again, because she could feel her breath catching, feel him hardening against her stomach…

Violet vowed to herself that if he didn't kiss her this second, she would walk away.

Fortunately, there was no need to walk away.

Because he answered her demand, his lips lightly brushing her own.

The soft contact was so welcome it almost made her startle, because it was all that had been missing. He cosseted her lips, indulged them tenderly till they were attuned to his. And then he delivered more…still soft, but a deeper peek at further treasures as his tongue met the tip of hers.

For Violet, this was usually the moment she involuntarily rebelled—the moment when her body shrilled because it was too close to another. Were she with another man right about now she'd revolt—pull her head back in alarm, press her lips closed. Tonight, though, or rather with Sahir, it felt exactly right and, closing her eyes, she found there was only the soft thrill of bliss, followed by a new and fervent desire to reciprocate.

I'm kissing, Violet thought as their mouths meshed softly. And he allowed her tongue to toy with his until she had to taste him more deeply and he obliged.

His hand moved to the back of her head, exerting a gentle pressure as his mouth took command. And the crush of his lips, the slow revelling of his tongue, had the fire that had been kindling in Violet igniting, shooting flame in directions she'd never so much as sought before.

She was by far too eager as her hands came to his hips, tugging at his shirt, desperate to feel his skin, yearning for a deeper taste. To be guided straight to more bliss.

Sahir must have felt her need for escalation, and yet he refused to reciprocate, or cave to her demand. Instead she felt the sure placement of his hands on her cheeks as he moved his mouth back.

'We're being called.'

'No.'

Oh, but they were—she could hear Carter's voice.

'Where's Sahir?'

They stood, foreheads resting on each other, as Grace joined in with the search.

'I have to say goodbye to Violet.'

There was no avoiding the world.

'Go that way.'

Sahir pointed to an exit she hadn't even seen.

'It will take you out by the restroom. And tidy up,' he told her, while tucking his shirt in, then straightening his tie 'I'll say I had to make a phone call.' He gave a wry laugh. 'Actually, I do.'

And then what? she wanted to ask, unsure if this was it—if a kiss was the only wish she'd be granted.

But rather than ask, she wiped her lip-gloss from his cheek... oh, and the other one. Gosh, even his chin.

Yes, she'd better go and tidy up!

And now, after such a nice kiss, she was being shown the red card.

'I'll say goodbye here…' Sahir told her.

'Okay.'

'I have appointments tomorrow, and then I fly…'

'You already said.'

There was a knock on the door they'd entered through, and as she slipped out through the other exit he took out his phone and started talking in Arabic.

Carter called his name, opening the door the moment she'd slipped away.

Damn.

She stood in the tiny bathroom, frantically smoothing her hair and toning down her cheeks.

She wasn't stinging from rejection—she'd grown up with it, refused to react… She was just annoyed that Sahir was doing what he considered the right thing by her.

What he didn't get was that she'd been waiting a long time to feel so right, so sure, so…

Damn.

Why did she have to get a decent bastard?

'There you are!'

Grace was smiling as Violet duly came out of the restroom, her lip-gloss back on, her smile in place, trying to act normal—as if her legs knew how to walk and she hadn't just glimpsed paradise.

'We're heading off,' Grace told her. 'Carter's just rounding up Sahir.' She rolled her eyes. 'I know he doesn't like me…'

'You don't know that.'

'He thinks it's all about money…' She looked at Violet then. 'You think so too.'

'Not any more,' Violet admitted, and gave her friend a hug. 'I love you, Mrs Bennett…'

'I love you too,' Grace told her, then whispered, 'Don't tell a soul…you're going to be an aunty…'

Violet tried not to squeal. Because even if she wasn't technically going to be an aunty, they were closer than many sisters and it was just the most wonderful news. So brilliant that even deep kisses and sexy Sahir were momentarily forgotten as the news sank in.

'I'm so happy…' She hugged Grace tighter. 'Oh, my, God…'

She felt dizzy, and then suddenly guilty that she'd been so wrong about them both. And as the party headed out to the waiting car, and she saw the smiles on the newlyweds' faces and realised that she'd been trusted with a precious secret, a huge wave of emotion hit her—a delectable moment when everything felt right in the world.

Indeed, one kiss was all Sahir would be granting. What a kiss, though…

The afternoon and evening had raced by, and the wedding had been made both interesting and fun—and fun wasn't something Sahir either sought or was particularly used to.

And now it would seem it was over, because duty had tried to call—the reason he'd had to slip off earlier, even though his phone was effectively off, save for one particular line.

'Did you find out who was trying to get hold of me?' he asked Pria.

'It was an error,' Pria told him. 'They were checking procedures for tomorrow.'

Reassured, he headed out to the street and stood on the other side of the carpet from Violet, hands in his pockets, watching Carter and Grace get into the car. He glanced down the street and saw Maaz a couple of doors down, and Layla in her car.

Very deliberately, he was doing all he could not to look at Violet.

Once the newlyweds had gone, he'd head back to the restaurant, wish Violet goodnight and then he would head home.

He could still smell Violet's meadowy scent on his jacket, still feel the slight sheen of her gloss on his mouth—or was that more a case of wishful thinking?

He was in no mood for a virgin.

Okay, he was very much in the mood for a certain virgin—but he was trying to do the right thing here.

Grace threw the bouquet, and—phew! Violet didn't even leap to catch it, instead that blond bastard caught it.

'Flowers for your wife!' Violet called out, and Sahir smothered a smile as she put him in his place for eyeing her up earlier.

Violet Lewis should write on her bio that she was independent and tough—that she knew what she wanted for her first time and losers need not apply.

Oh, and she could also add gorgeous and mind-altering too.

And sexy as hell.

There was a vulnerability to her too, though…

Sahir stood as the car containing the happy couple was driven off and some things never changed—of course he did not wave.

One thing had changed, though…

As they walked back into the restaurant he watched Violet reach for her purse. Somehow knew she wasn't going to linger just to be turned down…

'Violet?'

'Please.' She put up her hand. 'I don't need the farewell speech—'

'Violet,' he interrupted. 'I don't want tonight to end either.'

He adored the way her eyes widened.

'But I do fly home tomorrow, and as I said…'

'Oh, gosh…' She waved tomorrow away. 'I know all that. And Grace and Carter must never, ever know…'

'Agreed.' He smiled. 'I just have to get rid of some people.'

'Were you all meant to be going off to a club?'

'Something like that,' Sahir said, not wanting to burst this incredible bubble they'd found by talking about his protection officers or revealing his title. 'Can you wait for me in the garden?'

'Yes.'

Discreetly he slipped her the key. 'I shan't be long.'

Her eyes told him she'd wait...

CHAPTER FIVE

VIOLET TURNED THE key and stepped into the courtyard. Her heart hadn't stopped hammering since their kiss. He was the first person she'd truly coveted—the first person she'd felt an actual need for.

As someone who'd practically brought herself up it was new and unfamiliar.

She'd felt looked after by him from that moment outside the nursing home.

More, she'd been completely herself.

She'd hidden her tears and upset from Grace, dragged out her happy smile for her old schoolfriends, and then, when Tanya had been such a cow...

Her children had run wild, Violet thought, looking at the table full of half-unwrapped gifts.

She was checking that her box didn't rattle when her eyes caught sight of the most beautiful silver candelabra. As she went to pick it up she briefly wondered if it been secured somehow, because it barely moved, but then she realised she hadn't been expecting it to be so heavy...

Gosh, it was beautiful—seriously so.

She stared at it closely. The parts that caught the wax were different colours—one silver, one a rosy gold.

She sat on the little bench, still holding the candelabra. She was excited for the night and the adventure ahead. Okay, and a teeny bit nervous, Violet admitted. And she felt suddenly shy as he came through the wooden door.

'Running off with the silver?' he teased.

'I think my arm would fall off if I tried to run off with this.'

She both blushed and smiled, but his words hadn't hurt or offended, and she hadn't jumped as if she was being accused, as she so often did. Violet was simply pleased to see him.

'I was just admiring it.' She frowned then, remembering he'd said he'd bought them a candle stick. 'Is this your gift?'

Sahir nodded. 'It is…' He paused. 'Carter and I are working on a project together in Janana.'

'So, this is from your country?'

'Yes.'

'Gosh.' She went to hand it to him, but paused again to take in its absolute beauty. It was so solid, and yet so intricate. 'This part is different,' she said. She couldn't stop staring. 'The wax catcher. Perhaps they ran out of silver and had to use brass?'

It was rose gold, and the bobèches—or wax catchers, as Violet described them—depicted a full moon with Mars in opposition to the sun.

To Sahir's surprise he wanted to share that with Violet—to sit on the bench and tell her about the Setarah collection, even to describe the palace, how it was shaped like a star.

She tried to hand it to him, but it was truly heavy, and she pulled a funny face as he took the weight.

'Beats my tulip vase,' she said as he replaced it on the table, and then she stood.

'Here.' He gave her his jacket and suggested that instead of walking out through the restaurant they leave by the rear exit.

'Are you famous?' she asked as they walked down a cobbled side street. 'It's all very cloak and dagger.'

'In some circles.' He nodded. 'I guess you could say that.'

They walked along another beautiful street and then came

to a gate. She looked at the very smart house that backed onto a formal garden as he punched a code into the gate.

'You live here?' she checked as they walked through the garden and he entered another security code, and another...

'When we get in,' he said, 'if you just want a drink—'

'If you send me home after a drink I'll be *extremely* upset!'

She would—because for her whole life she'd been looked at as second rate. Sahir made her feel first rate.

Sahir would be her first.

Her eyes widened and then narrowed as she took in the size of his residence, frowning when she saw the dining table. 'Are those the same candle—?'

'Do you really want a tour?' he asked.

'No.' She laughed as they stepped into the lounge and she pointed to a decanter. 'But I'll have a glass of that.'

'Not if you're staying,' he said. 'I want us both to remember this...every last moment.'

She thought she should feel shy, but it had faded, and there was not even a glimpse of it.

The light of the moon was streaming in through the French doors and she looked out at a glorious balcony.

'Oh, my goodness...' she said.

Under any other circumstance she would have been tempted to step out, for the view of London must be stunning from there...but as he came and stood behind her there was something rather more vital occupying her attention.

He removed his jacket from her and kissed her shoulder, as he had in the courtyard, and instead of opening the French doors she turned around.

'Are you nervous?' he asked.

She considered his question, then she turned clear blue eyes to him. 'No.' She shook her head. 'I'm...'

She swallowed, because this felt so right, so perfect, that something told her it could only ever have been him. It was as if last weekend's date and every dreadful date she'd walked away from before had been mere signposts that had turned her away and somehow led her to a place she felt she perfectly belonged.

'I feel happy.'

'So do I.'

He brought her back into his embrace, as if they were dancing again, though he pulled her closer than he previously had, and his cheek was next to hers. This time she allowed her skin to rest on his and breathed him in. She closed her eyes as his mouth moved as she had wanted it to on the dance floor. It created a warm path to her lips, and she parted them.

His kiss was different from the one in the courtyard. There, she had felt restraint...now it was warm and slow. She wasn't fighting the feelings he evoked, just letting them ripple through her. Feeling the silk of his hair beneath her fingers and how her breasts ached as her arms reached behind him...how his hands on her hips guiding her in made her feel warm and aching down below.

So much so that she moaned into his mouth and briefly pulled back. 'Turns out I do like kissing.'

He smiled and got back to her mouth, and just for a moment he lost concentration. For it had dawned on him that he hadn't particularly been a fan of kissing either...

Or of feeling happy.

Until this night...

They stood staring at each other, mouths almost together, exchanging the sensual air. He touched the top of her arm and stroked it.

His touch made her hungry...it made her weak, it made her bold. She did something she never had before. She kissed his neck...ran her mouth over the scratchy throat that had been so smooth just hours ago. It made her desperate to see it dark and shadowed and rough in the morning.

'Careful,' he warned.

'I don't want to be careful,' she whispered, breathing into his sexy ear.

He adored every word, every moment, every taste of her skin and the feel of her awakening to him. He loved feeling her desire building and, yes, he wanted to be her first.

There were not enough hours in the night to do all that he wanted, but he wanted more of that laughter, more of everything…

There would be no sleeping tonight.

He wanted her shoes on his floor. He wanted her earrings by his bed, her perfume on his pillow and traces of her everywhere.

Taking her hand, he led her to the principal bedroom.

The covers were turned back, the side lamps on, and he removed her earrings very carefully.

'They're not expensive,' she said, because he was treating them with such care, placing them neatly by the bed.

And he wasn't shy either, because he went to the bedside table and saw her swallow as he took out some condoms and then lifted the lid on a small container.

'What's that?' she asked.

'Oil.'

'For me or you?'

'Both.'

She dipped in her fingers and the fragrance was like every season condensed on her fingers, so subtle.

'I don't think I need it,' she whispered, and he was aware of her own arousal. 'And as for them…' She pointed at the condoms. 'I'm on the pill. Or do you always use them?'

'Absolutely.'

There could be no chance of an unplanned pregnancy. He always wore a condom, to protect both himself and his partner.

Only this was something he had never encountered before.

A woman who wanted just him and just this.

So was it a kick of rebellion as he replaced the condoms in the drawer?

Or trust?

No, for he trusted no one.

And yet, here they stood, and he wanted every moment of this night, every inch of her naked skin.

He pulled her to him and found the little side zip of her dress.

'Violet…' he whispered—for, as she'd said the dress had been calling her, she had been calling to him all night.

It was pure silk, and it fell as such, and he loved her pale breasts and her little silver knickers. He removed them too, and then led her to a bedroom chair, where she sat, naked apart from her heels.

He removed his tie, and then his cufflinks. She was watching his every move intently. She reminded him of a little hawk, just learning to track.

She noted everything.

Every button and every glimpse of his chest made her own chest tighten.

He removed his shirt and Violet watched as his gorgeous chest was revealed. She felt her bottom lift a little from the chair.

He kicked off his shoes and then he came closer. He placed one foot on her thigh and wordlessly, wondrously, she rolled down the black sock, exposing one long, elegant foot even as his hand pulled all the pins from her hair. She stroked the coffee-coloured skin of the foot on her thigh and then he removed it.

She crossed her legs, as if it might somehow calm the now swollen flesh between her legs.

Sahir presented his second socked foot, and as she slipped the other sock off his hand was loosening her hair. Then the sole of his foot slid between her legs, prising her thighs apart as if he knew the turmoil she felt between them.

He was looking between her legs as he unbelted his trousers, then slipped down his zipper. She felt her legs pressing back together of their own volition—not to hide, just in unfamiliar tension—as he removed the last of his clothing and she saw him erect, saw the gorgeous dark silky hair. The excitement of his arousal made her weak…

'Stay there,' he said.

And she continued to sit as he knelt down and pulled her bottom to the edge of the chair. He stroked her whilst easing her legs further apart. She touched his broad shoulders a little tentatively, as if he might suddenly disappear.

'Why aren't I shy?' she asked.

'It's just us…you don't need to be.'

He kissed her breasts, and she felt nicely lazy as he ministered to each one, his tongue perfection in its light suction, the small nips of his teeth. And then his head trailed down, and she looked at her breasts, wet from his mouth and unfamiliar with their budded nipples.

Her stomach was kissed deeply, and she leant back in the hard chair and closed her eyes. Then she moaned as his fingers parted her and his tongue explored her and it was the nicest, most unhurried moment. She looked down and saw his black hair, felt the tension in his shoulders, while her legs were so limp that he easily lifted them over him.

'I should do something…'

It was the vaguest ever offer to help—like offering to do the almost done dishes. Because she never wanted to move again. He ignored her anyway, just caressed her with his mouth, with his lips and his tongue.

'Sahir…' she said, sensation rippling through her.

His mouth was taking all the tension of the day, until it faded away with a sigh.

'Oh…'

She smiled down at him, then closed her eyes, wishing there was a switch that might flip the chair so she could lie back, breathless and pleasure-filled…

But then he removed her legs from his shoulders and kissed her, his lips made shiny from her delectably gentle first orgasm. And then he held her chin and met her eyes.

'You're sure?'

'More than sure…'

That said, she gulped when she looked at him. For she had thought him erect before, but he was even bigger now. Considerably. He held the tip to where she was still tender, stroking her, wetting her a little, and she watched, her thighs aching, her throat tight with anticipation.

'We'll go to bed,' he said.

At first it seemed a helpful suggestion, and she nodded. 'This chair's not very—'

Only her words caught—for suddenly she didn't want him to stop, and she forgot about hard chair backs and protruding arms and everything. She was entranced, just watching him nudge a little inside her.

'Can we please stay here?'

He pulled her bottom a little closer to the edge, and she thought there was something heady about watching someone so strong and determined attempt and fail. Because as he hit resistance she tensed, and he careered a little to one side…

She reached down and felt the velvet of his skin, explored the veins. And then she just held him and stroked him.

'Bed,' he said.

But she liked them being here.

'No,' she insisted.

He closed a hand over her own, and as he nudged in again she couldn't help but voice the pain.

When he pulled out there was a little blood on his thick tip.

'Bed!'

Finally Violet agreed.

He scooped her up, and she had barely been lain down when he was over her. Violet's eager arms reached for him, holding his face as they kissed.

Sahir kissed her harder, making her mouth hot and swollen. He made her tongue dance with his and she felt him hard against her stomach and her pubic bone, moving lower. She felt the crush of his body as he kissed her neck. And then for the first time in her life Violet felt adored.

Utterly looked-after.

The most looked-after she'd ever felt.

'I am so glad it's you,' she said, putting her arms around his neck.

He answered in Arabic, and then his full lips hovered over her mouth. 'I am honoured that it is me.'

And now he took her, smothering her cries with his mouth, but she was ready. And he pushed through the last resistance… found her stretched, ready and, oh, so willing flesh.

The grip of her had his breath shuddering as his body fought for restraint. He held himself still within her as he kissed her slowly, hearing her low, throaty entreaties.

He was beyond logic now, and he drove in, closing his eyes in brief cognisance that he was bedding a virgin.

And he *was* bedding her.

'Sahir…'

She felt his hand slide to the small of her back, felt his stomach on hers, as if cradling the pressure within, as if absorbing it, giving her a moment to acclimatise, and when his mouth pulled back she watched his closed eyes open, knew they were both lost in themselves and yet so linked together.

He moved out a little and she pressed her lips tight, as if braced for the next push. She hummed as he slid in deeper, then nodded as he did the same again, only more precisely this time. Her thighs were shaking. Without intention she tried to wrap her legs around him—and promptly failed.

'I'm so unfit,' she admitted.

He laughed. She hadn't heard him laugh in that way, and it was as low and as sexy as the man himself. He took her leg and pushed it back further, and she did the same with the other leg. He took her with hard thrusts that made her weak, this glimpse of unbridled need both exciting and thrilling her.

'I want you wrapped around me,' he told her, and her less than agile legs attempted to do it again.

Nothing could prise her off him now, because he thrust, and then thrust again, and there was another glimpse of him, a surge of rawness that had her wanting more, and they were locked together...

He felt her breasts against his chest, her legs tight around his hips and her hands in his hair. It wasn't the smooth sex he was used to—it wasn't anything he was used to...

Sahir pulled the pillow out from beneath her head, and Violet felt as if there might be no mattress—because she was in freefall.

She felt the wave of her second orgasm, not at all comparable to the little butterflies she'd felt whilst on the chair. It was all-consuming. Her legs slipped away, joined by the delicious sensation of him rigid for a second before he achieved his own release.

'That was heavenly,' Violet told him, and it would seem he agreed. Because he came down by her side and pulled her into him and they just caught their breath.

'Are you okay?' he asked.

'About what?'

'You're not going to have major regrets?'

'Gosh, no.'

She felt as if the world had been put right. As if her every last hang-up had been taken care of. Every fear about men, sex, life…all were vanquished, at least for now.

'Though Grace must never, ever know.'

Violet let out a laugh that made him smile.

'We'll nod politely if we meet…'

Then she fell quiet.

Sahir was silent too.

Everything would be different when they next met, he knew.

Soon Grace would tell her of his royal status, or she'd find out for herself. Perhaps it was better that she heard that at least from him.

'I have appointments tomorrow.'

'I know…' Violet sighed. 'What time am I being kicked out?'

'Not yet.'

'Will we do it again?'

Sahir half laughed and pulled her closer, so her head was on his chest, and she lay there, feeling as contented as she ever had.

'Tomorrow night I fly to Janana,' he told her.

'You said.'

She played with the gorgeous hair on his stomach. She loved lying relaxed and naked in his arms, half asleep and simply talking—it was another new adventure for Violet, and she loved the lulling of his low voice.

'Carter does some work there?' she checked.

'Yes.'

'Rebuilding some ancient palace.' She stroked the lovely black hair. 'Are you working on it with him?'

'I am. I studied historical architecture.'

Her voice was sleepy, yet she didn't want to give in, wanted every minute of their night. 'Is that the same as what Carter does?'

'No, he's an architect.'

* * *

He thought of the years it had taken to get to this point with the project.

'It's a very ancient structure,' he told her.

'Mmm…'

'One wing was destroyed in an earthquake more than a century ago. There are a lot of people opposed to disturbing the ruins.'

If she hushed him, he'd say no more, Sahir decided.

'How come?'

'Many were killed—including the then Queen.'

He felt her stir of interest, the way her thigh moved across him, how her head moved a little, as if her ears had pricked up in curiosity.

'The King fell into deep grief…he killed himself a couple of weeks later.'

'Goodness.'

'There was a lot of turmoil in the country. A new king had to be appointed, with a whole new lineage. Rules were put in place so it could never happen again.'

'You can't prevent an earthquake.'

'I mean rules to ensure that a king could never again jeopardise his country's future because of his personal emotions.'

'You can't stop—'

'There is no love allowed in a royal marriage.' He stared at the ceiling. 'It must be a purely business arrangement.'

'Wow…' She seemed to ponder that for a moment. 'Are there bodies still buried in the ruins?'

'No.' He found that he'd smiled at her question, squeezed her arm in affectionate rebuke. 'Your thoughts are very dark.'

'Oh, yes.'

He felt her relax back into him.

'So, what happens now?' she asked.

'We are waiting for the council to approve the plans.'

'Well, if it's anything like our local council…'

'No!' He gave a half-laugh. He knew she was teasing, yet she made the serious subject a little lighter, made him want to explain their curious ways.

Her breathing was slowing and her eyes were closing, he was sure, but then she jolted herself awake, and he wanted to make love to her all over again.

But first…

If he didn't want her to hear it from Grace…

Sahir made himself say it.

'The new wing of the palace is where I shall reside…'

He felt her jolt again, saw the raising of her head from his chest, and then he heard her question.

'When?'

'When I am King.'

CHAPTER SIX

'KING?' VIOLET STARTED to laugh.

Sahir didn't.

Her eyes were wide open now and she actually sat up. 'So, you're a prince?'

'The Crown Prince.'

'Crikey.'

'A few hours from now I have a function to attend, then I fly back to Janana later that night.'

'Oh.' She stared at him. 'I honestly don't know what to say.'

'I am just trying to explain that I have to leave and why I—'

She put a hand to his mouth. 'You don't have to explain the next part.'

'What next part?'

'That I'm a very unsuitable date for a future king.'

'You'd be a wonderful date, but…'

Unsuitable in ways she could not begin to comprehend.

He had told her more than he'd ever told any other woman, and he already felt close to her in ways the laws strictly dictated he avoid, but… 'I'm needed back home.'

'I get it. Well…' She frowned. 'Of course, I don't…'

Violet turned on the light.

'What are you doing?'

'I knew there was something.'

She didn't sound daunted or overwhelmed. Truly just thrilled to have spent the night with him.

'Something?' Sahir checked.

'You're so formal…' She pinched his nipple. 'When you're not being sexy.'

He caught her wrist and held it there, and looked up at those blue eyes smiling down at him.

And nothing—not a thing—had changed.

'Come here,' he told her, taking her head and pulling it down to his.

There would be no sleeping tonight…

None.

At dawn he ran them a bath, and Violet rather gingerly climbed in so that she faced him.

'Ouch, ouch, ouch…' she said, lowering herself down, and then sinking into the relief of the warm water. 'You have chased this horrible week away,' she told him as she soaped his chest. 'Honestly, when I look back I am going to smile now, and remind myself there's always a silver lining…'

'Good.'

It was his turn with the soap now. He washed first her arms, her hands, her fingers, and then he washed her breasts.

He moved her onto his lap…

But even as they kissed the world was waking up—his phone was bleeping from the bedroom.

'Ignore it…' she told him.

Sahir was tempted to bolt all entrances.

'Violet…'

She looked up, wrapped in a towel and gathering up her clothes.

'Stay for breakfast.'

'There are people arriving…'

'I know. Look, I can't miss today.'

'I get that.'

And Violet absolutely did. He was the person who was leaving, the man who could never be, and right now that thought didn't scare her. She had never dared so much as to hope for even one such wonderful, magical night and Sahir had given her that.

'I know you're busy.'

'Yes. However, would you like to spend the day here?'

'Why?'

'I don't want you to feel I'm rushing off. I can delay the flight…we can have a late dinner tonight—only this time without so much company.'

She knew what he meant. As wonderful as the whole night had been, for Violet, the best moments had been those spent alone with him.

'Just us,' he added.

'I'd love that.'

Violet needed little persuading. She had thought goodbye was imminent, and she accepted the reprieve with delight.

'I have to get dressed,' he told her.

'It's a bit late to be shy,' Violet said, and smiled, but then he explained he had someone coming in to assist him.

'Formal attire,' he said.

'Oh!'

While she wasn't in the least embarrassed with Sahir, she was not going to sit around with someone else here.

Before he let someone called Faisal in, she pulled on her gorgeous silk gown, then opened the French windows and stepped onto the balcony, feeling the gorgeous breeze… A helicopter was hovering in the blue, blue sky and she stretched her arms up and arched her neck, then gazed out at the new and beautiful morning.

How long she stood there, Violet wasn't sure. She was just daydreaming, and reliving the night they'd shared.

'Hey…'

She turned and caught her breath. Sahir wore a white robe and his *kafir* was tied with gold braid. He looked magnificent.

'Look at you…'

'I was just enjoying looking at *you*,' he responded. 'Your breakfast is here.'

It was the most beautiful Sunday she had ever known, Violet decided as she swapped her hired gown for a robe and climbed into bed.

Sahir placed a tray across her lap.

'I might watch a movie,' she said, buttering a muffin with jam. But then, glancing around, she saw there was no television. 'Or sleep…'

He picked up a little remote, and a huge screen popped up as if from the end of the bed.

'Anything you need, just use the phone.'

'Does it work for Florentines?' she teased.

'It works for anything.'

'Do I get a kiss?'

'No.' He looked at her strawberry-jam-covered fingers and lips. 'But I'll make up for that tonight.'

'Good luck, then,' she said, and gave him a smile. 'Hurry back!'

Sahir left her in a cloud of white linen, working her way through a pot of tea.

He swept downstairs and spoke with Faisal about dinner—and arranged for a treat to be delivered to her.

As he went to leave, Sahir paused. Last night had been incredible. Not just the sex, but the before and after. He simply could not imagine sitting down to dinner with Violet tonight and boarding his jet straight afterwards. Certainly she deserved more than that—and, most rarely for Sahir, he wanted more of a lover's company…

For the last two years he had worked non-stop—in contrast

with his younger brother, Ibrahim, who did very little, and his sister, Jasmine, who did… Well, nothing much at all.

While Sahir had certainly lived a decadent life at times, duty had always outweighed everything else. Perhaps it was time for his siblings to step up when required.

Because right now, Sahir felt more time with Violet was required.

Life was going to be hectic once he returned, and while he knew Violet should be spending this week looking for work, he did want to indulge her and mark the preciousness of last night.

In the dining room, his escorts were waiting, and as Faisal made the final adjustments to his *kafir* he spoke with Pria.

'I am going to be staying in London for another week. Can you make the necessary arrangements?'

'Sir…?' Aadil glanced over. 'We are scheduled to depart tonight.'

'The schedule has changed,' Sahir responded.

Certainly he didn't need to explain his reasons, simply order it to be arranged.

Still, as he got into the waiting vehicle, Sahir knew that the sudden delay to his return would already be causing a stir— both amongst his staff here in London and at the palace in Janana.

That was quickly confirmed when, moments later, a call came through from the King.

'Another week in London?' he snapped.

'Correct,' Sahir told his father. 'Thanks to the delays with the council over the palace refurbishment, I have a clear schedule.'

'King Abdul has asked for a meeting. I was relying on you to take it.'

'You have three heirs. Ibrahim or Jasmine can step up.'

'Jasmine gets too worked up.'

'I'm aware.'

'And your brother is on vacation.'

Again? Sahir was tempted to say, but instead he offered a more personal response. 'So am I.'

Yes, he was taking a vacation—his first week off in more than one hundred—and God it felt good.

'I have to go now,' Sahir informed his father.

As the car moved forward to enter the formal procession Sahir ended the conversation with the courtliness expected of him.

'Your Majesty.'

Violet completely *loved* not being a virgin!

Especially so when sitting propped up on cushions in Sahir's sumptuous bed, eating the Florentines that had been served on a pretty plate!

'Where on earth…?' Violet had blinked when they'd arrived, then been told His Highness had arranged a delivery.

The only thing she had to worry about was deciding which movie to watch.

She flicked happily past all the news channels—misery had no place in this day. But then something, or rather *someone*, caught Violet's attention and she quickly flicked back.

'It's me!' she gasped.

It really was!

Florentines forgotten, Violet stared at herself on screen. Her head was thrown back and both arms stretched out, as if in salutation to the glorious morning. Her gorgeous gown billowed in the morning breeze.

Oh, she wished she could record the image—because it captured precisely how happy she felt, how perfect.

'A glorious London morning,' the plummy newsreader was saying. 'And for our viewers just joining us, let's take a quick look back—these are the first arrivals, making their way down The Mall.'

'Oh, who cares?' Violet muttered. 'Get back to me.'

But then, realising that Sahir might be in one of the cars on screen, she found that she did care after all, and started trying to work out who was who.

However, she was vain enough to smile in delight when the camera cut back to her.

'Somebody is clearly enjoying the view...' the newsreader said.

They were talking about her, Violet realised as the camera zoomed in on the balcony. But her brief revelling in celebrity vanished, vanity forgotten, and her breath caught as on the screen the most beautiful man in the world stepped through the French windows. It was Sahir, *kafir* on, wearing his formal robes, and looking as delectable as ever.

Then they were back to the cars.

Was it vanity or lust that had her scouring the internet trying to find more images of them?

Violet wanted that moment captured, wanted it saved on her phone, but it was nowhere to be found.

She hit rewind on the news channel, tried to go back fifteen minutes...ten...thirty. But there was nothing...

'Where am I?' she muttered.

She tried for ages, but found nothing, so she lay back in bed, sulking but happy, watching all the dignitaries arrive. Her eyes were growing heavy at the presenter's drone, yet she fought to keep them open in the hope of catching a glimpse of Sahir.

But there was no sign of him, and after such a brilliant night of dancing, talking and being so gloriously 'bedded'—as Sahir would say—her lack of sleep was finally catching up.

She lay curled up in the bed, excited at the prospect of Sahir coming back this evening. She'd honestly thought she'd be back in her little flat by now...

Her bravado wavered a fraction as she slid towards slumber. She'd known all they had was one night... But the thought of stepping into her empty flat and peeling off her dress... Even the prospect of a week off work didn't help—she'd rather be there, be busy...

Instead, she'd be returning her dress. Looking for a job.

She thought of what Sahir had said last night.

'We all have our own mountain to climb.'

Violet half wondered about his. Certainly, she'd faced many mountains in her time—starting over with a new family, saying goodbye to her own. New people…new faces… Endless goodbyes and people walking away.

With Sahir it felt different.

Her heavy eyelids fluttered open in a brief attempt to face this new mountain she was about to climb, yet she was daunted by the prospect of saying goodbye to Sahir.

The little mountain seemed to have turned into the Alps—only they weren't inviting. They were icy and cold, with dark clouds hiding their peaks. And, really, she didn't want to know what was up there.

She glimpsed missing Sahir, getting over their wonderful night, facing a whole world without him…

Violet had a very good trick for when panic hit.

She hid.

Pulling the crisp linen over her head, she closed her eyes and gave in to the bliss of sleep.

Sahir rarely missed a beat at these events.

Yet today he struggled to focus on his conversations, and Pria had to subtly prompt him to offer his condolences to the Sultan.

Certainly, the Sultan didn't get the extended, effusive words of sympathy that Aadil had suggested…

For the first time Sahir just wanted this over and to head home.

Not *home*, home…

But back to his bolthole in London, where Violet was waiting.

'Your Highness…' As he mingled in the grounds, Pria discreetly pulled him aside. 'There might be a slight issue.'

He frowned.

'Some footage of your balcony was briefly aired on television. Aadil was straight on it and it's been taken down.'

'I see.' Sahir immediately understood the concern. 'Was it just my guest the cameras captured?' he enquired.

Sahir wouldn't be so crass as to look at his phone in the current surrounds.

'Layla has the footage. She thinks you might have been glimpsed, although there's no sign of you on anything else we've seen...' She glanced to her own assistant, Kumu, who shook her head in agreement. 'As I said, sir,' Pria continued, 'it's all been taken down, and Aadil is going to speak to your guest and ensure that she doesn't go back out onto the balcony.'

'I would prefer for you to be the person to speak with her,' Sahir said. He knew Aadil would be by far too abrupt, and that Pria would be tactful and kind. 'Kumu can take over here.'

'Sir...' Pria said, and she swallowed.

Sahir was aware that Kumu was new and it was her first foreign trip.

'We'll be fine.' Sahir nodded. 'Let me know if there are any updates.'

There were none.

The reception was magnificent, the company interesting at times, but even so, for Sahir, the day seemed to move at a ridiculously slow pace.

It had nothing to do with the lack of sleep—it was his mind all too often drifting to the night ahead, to last night...

It was most unlike Sahir, but he even found his gaze wandering, looking for Pria. Or even Aadil.

He just wanted to know that Violet was okay.

Finally the formalities were over, and he was more than relieved to climb into his private vehicle, with both Kumu and Layla joining him.

'Where's Pria?' He frowned.

'I'm not sure,' Layla admitted.

'I sent her to the house a while ago. What about Aadil...?'

'I haven't seen him. I had a message to say that all the footage has been taken down, though there's the occasional photo popping up...'

Of course she had them stored, and Sahir glanced at the photo on Layla's phone and had to force himself not to take it from her just to get a better look. Actually, he had to force himself not to smile—for there was Violet, just as he recalled seeing her this morning, only this was an aerial shot.

'Hardly incriminating,' he said.

He'd been over and over that moment in his head, and aside from that, Sahir always took great care.

'What about the footage?' he asked, and Layla handed him the phone and he played the short video.

Violet stood there, her face turned to the skies, her arms waving as if she was standing on the bow in the *Titanic* movie, looking so wonderful and free.

And for the rest of the week he would be too.

'Oh,' Kumu said. 'The King is asking you to call him.' Her eyes were wide with alarm, and she was clearly struggling with Pria's tablet. 'The request came through an hour ago.'

'It's fine,' Sahir said, quietly certain that his father wanted to discuss the futility of sending an unversed Ibrahim or a nervous Jasmine to meet with King Abdul.

God, it had been a long day...

He glanced out of the window and realised the car had barely moved. Pressing a button, he opened the screen between himself and the driver.

'What's the delay?'

'We're just about to exit, sir.'

There were many other dignitaries leaving, and as they left the official event and blended into the traffic the crowds slowly started to disperse, with pedestrians ignoring traffic signals and crossing roads en masse.

'We're still well ahead of schedule,' Layla added, perhaps noticing that the usually measured Crown Prince was impatiently drumming the fingers of his free hand on the armrest.

Sahir halted the small gesture, for he rarely allowed his body to betray his thoughts or emotions.

Anyway, Layla was wrong. Sahir wasn't worrying about the schedule—he was feeling restless in the slow-moving vehicle. Or rather, he felt a sense of impatience building. He had a previously unknown desire to get home and tell Violet he'd taken the week off, work out what they might do with this precious slice of time he had engineered.

Sahir closed his eyes for a moment and arched his neck to one side as Kumu read through the messages that had piled up in his brief absence. He thought of Violet's smile when he told her tonight over dinner that they would be spending the week together. And then his mind drifted to how he'd left her, sitting in his bed, her lips and fingers sticky with jam, and it was not his taste buds that needed satisfying…

The kiss he'd been forced to deny her this morning would be delivered. More, if the house he was returning to was empty. He wanted to be messaging Violet now, warning her of his desirous approach. And he knew she would be there to greet him. Were it just the two of them, he doubted they'd make it up the stairs…

'Your Highness?' Kumu said. 'The council is being convened.'

Yes, Sahir thought. Now he'd taken a week off, suddenly they wanted to discuss his project.

They were pulling up at his residence. Maaz's unmarked car was blocking the entrance to the basement garage, but Sahir barely noticed it as he stepped onto the street.

'Your Highness,' Faisal greeted him. 'Is it possible…?'

'Later,' Sahir said.

He didn't want to discuss menus or such things now.

'Your Highness, forgive me...' Faisal persisted.

But Sahir was already opening the door to the principal bedroom.

'Violet?'

He frowned at the wall of silence that met him as he stepped in. The bed was made, her shoes and gown were gone, and he walked into the bathroom and saw it had been serviced.

'Where's my guest?' he asked, his voice bewildered as Faisal came to the door.

Layla was just behind him, her face pale. 'I just heard...' she said to Faisal, then addressed Sahir. 'Unfortunately, those images were seen.'

'I don't care about that now.' He turned to Faisal. 'Was my guest asked to leave? I specifically told Pria to be tactful.'

It was Faisal who spoke then. 'Aadil spoke with Miss Lewis before Pria arrived. It would seem the King had discussed matters with the elders and together with Aadil they all agreed...'

'Agreed to what?'

'That any further conversation should take place back in Janana.'

'And in due time it shall. Right now, I would like to speak with my guest...'

His patience was fast running out. The thought of Violet being bundled out of his home by Aadil incensed him. Violet deserved better than that.

'I need her address...'

He frowned at the intrusion as Maaz came bounding up the stairs. He nodded to Layla, as if confirming something, then cleared his throat.

'Sir, I have some information.'

'And?'

'The King felt that the situation was too volatile to leave your guest here...'

'I can see that.'

The room was empty, not even a trace of her perfume was

in the air, and though he appeared outwardly unmoved he was cursing himself for not getting her number, or even her address.

'You have her details...' He looked to Layla. 'She would have been vetted.'

'Sir.' It was poor Faisal who told him at last. 'Your guest has been taken to Janana...'

'Taken?' Sahir checked, unsure he'd heard right, for his pulse was pounding in his ears.

'The royal jet took off an hour ago,' Faisal confirmed.

It was beyond comprehension that his father, the King, would sanction this.

'Where's Pria?' he asked.

'She went with her, sir. I believe she thought it for the best...'

Violet must be terrified. He thought he had left her safe, instead—

'I need...' Sahir halted.

He must not reveal his frantic thoughts, nor his overwhelming need to see her.

'Arrange a flight,' he told Kumu. His voice was not his own, for it sounded measured rather than raw, his orders imperious, even as he reminded himself how to breathe. 'Tell the palace I shall be arriving tonight, and that I trust my guest is being made most welcome and has been allocated the Inanna wing.'

The Inanna wing—or Venus wing—was reserved for the most esteemed female guests, and in allocating it to Violet he was letting the palace know the high regard in which he held her and that she was to receive only the best.

The dreadful news didn't end there, though.

'Your Highness, Miss Lewis isn't at the palace.'

Faisal's voice seemed to be coming from a long way off, for Sahir's mind really was in too many places.

'I beg your pardon?'

'Miss Lewis isn't at the palace, sir,' Faisal said again, doing his best to hold his head high as he attempted to meet Sahir's eyes. 'Your guest has been taken to the desert abode.'

Sahir felt as if a cricket bat had struck the back of his head.

Violet really had been taken.

CHAPTER SEVEN

VIOLET WAS VERY good at giving herself pep talks.

You've been through worse.

All through this terrifying, bewildering day she had said those words to herself over and over, and now, deep in the night and even deeper in the desert, she told herself the same thing...

You've been through worse.

And she had been.

As a child, she'd been taken from her bed at night by social workers, arriving in a new foster home as an emergency placement.

She'd become used to it, really. Had come to accept the constant upheavals.

Today's events hurt at a different level.

She'd learned that Crown Prince Sahir of Janana was soon to be married!

Aadil and Pria had left, and now Violet sat on a jade velvet cushion, the two maids she had been left with staring at her...

Actually, they had been very sweet.

A little unsure what to do with their unexpected guest, they had held out robes, but Violet had turned her face away.

A little later they had led her to a beautiful bathing area, parting lavish drapes, and she saw they had drawn her a scented bath. But even though she ached to climb in and let the water absorb some of her tension, Violet had again shaken her head.

The older maid had moved to undo her zip. 'No!' Violet

had said abruptly, and then shooed them out. Actually, seeing her crestfallen face, Violet had felt dreadful for doing that, but she'd really needed the loo. She'd also filled the pretty basin with water and washed her hands and face, then stared at her reflection.

Through it all she hadn't cried.

Not once.

Violet never cried.

Well, she had yesterday, and Sahir had wiped away her tears…

She'd trusted him then.

For the first time in her life she'd completely trusted some-one.

Never again.

Never, ever…

When she'd returned to her cushion the maids had brought out endless refreshments, but again she had declined, shaking her head and drinking only water.

By now she'd worked out their names. Bedra was the older lady, and Amal seemed to be around Violet's age.

They both seemed concerned, and now they had unearthed a wooden trunk, holding up some English books.

'No, thank you,' she said.

Bedra, the older one, frowned.

'Laa,' Violet tried.

She knew a very few words of Arabic from her work in the library, but then she remembered one of her clients telling her that simply saying no—*laa*—could sound abrupt.

She reminded herself that it wasn't their fault she was here.

It was Sahir's.

'Laa, shukran,' Violet declined, more politely, and Bedra gave her a smile.

Then she gestured to Amal to help her carry the trunk into what were to be Violet's sleeping quarters.

Oh, yes.

Because when a nervous Pria had earlier shown her the Crown Prince's lavish sleeping area, Violet had loudly demanded an area of her own.

Pria had apologised, and started to cry, and Violet wasn't proud of causing her tears.

Gosh, she'd really been a rather demanding unexpected guest!

Now she sat bolt upright, her ears strained for any sound, her wary eyes taking in every detail of her luxurious surroundings. From the bells that tinkled softly as she entered an area or left one, to the lavish rugs that dulled her footsteps. The jewelled daggers and swords on display had been noted, as well as the heavy, thick rope that hung over the velvet-draped bed where presumably Sahir slept.

She heard a sound—a low hum, steadier than the erratic wind.

She saw Bedra sit up straight, then abruptly stand. Amal moved quickly too. As the sound drew closer she was lighting lamps and stoking the central fire, as Bedra lit incense and filled two silver goblets with wine.

Then she heard the jangle of bells, and Bedra speaking urgent words she didn't understand. But her gestures and meaning were clear.

His Highness is here. Stand. Hurry, you must stand.

Never.

Never, ever...

But then she saw the confusion and urgency in Bedra's eyes, and knew that to sit as he entered would embarrass her and cause great offence. So Violet pushed herself up from the cushion, watching the drapes part, expecting a stranger.

An arrogant, ruthless stranger who had hurt her right to her core.

But she held back a gasp when she saw the same man who had left her this morning, dressed in the same robes.

It was the same Sahir.

His robes were less pristine, his *kafir* was gone and his complexion had a grey tinge, and when he saw her she saw a spark of something in his eyes that looked like relief.

On the maids' quiet urging she briefly bowed her head, then returned her gaze to his.

Violet was standing.

Sahir had considered more than a thousand ways he might find her.

Sobbing on a bed, frantic with panic or even lunging at him in crazed anger.

Not once—not even for a second—had he expected to be met with such dignity.

Her blonde hair was tousled, her silk gown somewhat crushed, but she looked as elegant and beautiful as she had last night, as captivating as when she had climbed from that taxi. She looked angry, rather than scared, but pale, and her lips were white, her blue eyes glinting as if they were striking flint.

She *was* scared, though. Of that he was certain.

'Are you okay?'

It was possibly the most ridiculous question, because nothing about this was okay, but he wanted to deal with the practical first.

She didn't answer.

'Violet…' He inhaled deeply, dragging air into lungs that in recent hours had felt too taut to breathe. Seeing her again, he wanted so badly to reach for her, to take her in his arms, yet protocol did not allow for that and her stance warned him not to, for she stood ramrod-straight.

'I apologise.'

He saw her blink, and young Amal seemed to start a little. Perhaps he should have cleared the room first.

'I have just come from the palace. I spoke briefly with the King and his aide. It would seem there has been a misunderstanding.'

'Sahir…' She put up a hand and corrected herself. 'Your Highness.'

For the first time she used his title, though he knew that the courtesy was not for his benefit, but for the maids. Her voice was clear and determined, but it held the tiniest tremble, which she seemed to swallow down.

'May we speak alone?' she asked.

'Of course.'

But there were certain traditions, and Bedra approached with a goblet for him. He nodded and took it.

He watched as Amal handed Violet a goblet too.

'*Shukran,*' she said, and he was surprised to hear her thank Amal in Arabic.

'She has taken no refreshment,' Bedra informed him quietly.

He nodded, and though he knew they should both drink now, then replace the goblets on the tray, he saw Violet made no attempt to do so. Downing his wine, he replaced his own goblet and asked the maids to leave.

They stood there, staring silently as they heard the bells, and then softer bells, as the women made their way to the far end of the abode and finally they were alone.

'What happened?' he asked.

'You know damn well.'

'No, I want to hear it from you. I want to know all that occurred.'

'I was kidnapped!' Violet shouted, tossing her wine into the fire and throwing down the goblet—possibly the first person ever to display raw emotion in a royal abode. 'That's what "occurred".'

'There was a misunderstanding—' he started, but again she put up her hand.

'Please don't,' Violet interrupted. 'I have three things I would like to say…'

A sound from outside the tent halted her, and as he listened to the sound of the helicopter taking off he knew her planned speech had been thwarted.

'We shan't be leaving tonight…' he began.

Once more she put up her hand to halt him.

'Then that leaves me with two things I have to say.' She took a breath, as if running through a speech in her head, then lifted her gaze to his. 'Do you remember me telling you that this dress is a rental—due back tomorrow?'

Sahir frowned deeply. She had been taken to another country, whisked off to the desert, and she was worried about a dress? She *really* was like no one he had ever met.

'Can we not worry about the dress?'

'I *am* worried—and not just about my deposit. I gave them my word that it would be back.'

She was, to his bewilderment, clearly distraught about the gown.

'It's for a wedding!'

'I'll sort out the damned dress!' he told her.

'Oh, you'd better. I won't have you ruining that woman's dream day the same way you ruined our night.'

She took a breath, and he knew the damage that had been done. He would rectify that, Sahir swore to himself, but right now he'd deal with her list.

'What else?'

'You're engaged.'

'Who told you that?'

'The same man who told me there had been a security breach and we had to leave your house immediately.'

Sahir wanted details, but she told him very little.

'Adal…?'

'Aadil.' His jaw hardened, but his anger would not help matters. 'Tell me more.'

'No. Ask the relevant staff. Because I don't report to you, Sahir.'

She stood so strong, refusing to give him anything—not even a glimpse of the woman who had cried before his eyes, who had laughed and danced in his arms.

'Especially when you haven't answered my question. Are you to marry soon?'

'Apparently so.'

Sahir was not being deliberately evasive, but the mist of panic that had hit him was lifting a little, and while he did not understand all that had occurred, he knew Aadil's unexpected arrival in London should have been a sign, as well as the fact that the council had been convened.

'It's a yes or no answer, Sahir.'

A smile almost ghosted his lips at her demand for a straightforward answer. It was not the time to explain the intricate laws and the mysterious ways of his land, but neither would he lie.

'Yes.'

'I abhor violence...' Violet stepped forward. 'And I've always said there's no excuse for it—whatever the circumstance. Even so, never say never!'

She slapped his cheek.

He could have stopped her—he had reflexes like lightning and was the most skilled warrior—yet he let the slap land before catching her wrist. He'd allow her to have that one...and not just because he deserved it, but because now he had contact.

He could feel her pulse hammering beneath his fingers. Knew that despite appearances she was not just furious but petrified. And, yes, again he inhaled her fear...

'Violet...'

His voice halted, but not because he was without words. Just with the simple act of her reclaiming her hand, all they had shared—all the laughter and affection and trust, everything so easily built—had dissolved and he fought for its return.

'You're safe,' he told her.

'How can you even say that?'

'I swear you are safe.'

'I shall never forgive you,' Violet promised.

For the first time since arriving he saw the shimmer of tears, and he could feel not just her terror but her devastation.

'You slept with me, and now I find out that you're getting married.'

He reached for her. 'It's not how it seems…'

'Don't!'

She took back her wrist, turned and walked away.

'Where are you going?' he demanded.

Not only was he not used to anyone walking away from him, he had thought there was much more to discuss. As well as that, she was walking towards the music area.

'To bed,' she told him.

'That is the musicians' area.'

'Not just for musicians…' She threw the words over her shoulder as she walked off. 'Pria gave me a tour. She called it your "entertainment area".' She was shouting again now. 'I believe she meant it's where members of your harem await their summons.'

'Yes, had I lived a century ago.'

'Bedra showed me the cord above your bed.'

And now, instead of storming off to bed, she abruptly changed direction, taking a dagger from one of the walls.

He watched as she crossed the tent.

He didn't follow, but knew full well what she was doing. The ancient bells in the musicians' area jangled as she went into his sleeping quarters and cut through the cord over his bed. That was followed by a whip-like noise from above as the velvet was severed.

'Sorted,' she said, walking out again. 'And for your information, I don't answer to bells.'

'I would never expect you to.'

She marched into the musicians' room—her sleeping area.

'Violet, we need to—'

'I don't want to.'

'You need to eat.'

'Don't tell me what I need,' she said from behind the partition. 'I'm going to get some sleep.'

'Let me at least have the dress so I can send it back…'

He almost instantly regretted his suggestion when, through the fabric partition, he saw that she was stripping off.

Violet was correct that this room had once been where the harem awaited its summons.

But now Sahir came here for deep reflection, and always alone.

It was also where the monarch came after his wedding, or when the teller had informed the council that the time was ripe for an heir.

It was subtly erotic by design.

He turned his back, but her near naked shadow danced on the far wall.

So he looked up at the ceiling.

More Violets. A kaleidoscope of Violets, all dancing naked across the walls of the tent.

He examined his thumbnails until she threw out the violet dress.

'That needs to be urgently sorted,' she told him. 'You had better not let *another* bride down.'

'I don't have a bride.' He took a breath. 'Here, a royal marriage is very different. I don't even know who she'll—'

'La-la-la!' she shouted.

Here, that meant, 'No, no, no.' He knew what she meant, though, for he could see her shadow covering its ears, and also that whatever she wore it was see-through…

'Violet…'

Should he tell her she was as good as naked?

She'd soon work it out.

'I am going to go to—'

'Hell!' she finished for him, and Sahir knew there was no chance of reasonable conversation tonight.

He should leave things for now; they could speak tomorrow.

Her anger he accepted.

What he could not accept was the certain knowledge that she was scared.

And from what Bedra had told him she was probably hungry too.

Finally, there was something he could do.

Although perhaps not very well…

Violet didn't know where he was—just that he had gone.

She poured some water from the jug by the bed and drank a glass down, and as her temper left her she shivered.

Away from the fire it was cold, and the flimsy muslin nightdress that had been left out for her offered no warmth.

The wind was shrieking outside, and suddenly she was shaky. It was as if she'd held on to her nerve since the moment she'd realised she was being taken, and only now was her terror surfacing.

Now that *he* was here.

Bedra had left a few of the books by the bedside, and Violet had just climbed into the bed with one when Sahir spoke to her from the other side of the flimsy wall.

'I've brought you a drink and something to eat,' he said.

'I don't want it.'

'I'll bring it in.'

'Please don't.'

He ignored her, and she lay staring up at him as he walked in with a tray.

'So, no privacy?'

'I won't enter here again unless asked,' he said, moving the jug and glass, replacing them with a small plate and a tall red glass with ornate silver handles. 'You can hate me if you want, but you need to eat. I made some—'

'*You* made?' she sneered.

He looked down at her where she lay. 'That face you just pulled doesn't suit you.' He curled the side of his top lip. 'You look like a camel!'

She gave a shocked gasp. 'How rude.'

'Just an observation. And as for your supper…? I did make it—well, I made the drink.'

She turned and looked at the silver plate.

'I cannot take credit for the *gaz*,' he told her. 'It is very sweet…like nougat.'

She turned her head and stared straight ahead.

'I am going to go to the stables now.'

Please don't go, she wanted to say. But she didn't want to admit to Sahir how nervous she was at the thought of being here alone.

'I shouldn't be long. But there's a satellite phone there, and if I am to sort out the dress…'

'And a helicopter?'

'The wind is too high now to fly safely tonight,' he responded. 'The pilot was hesitant to bring me out—that is why the helicopter returned so quickly.' He looked at her for a moment. 'We can discuss all that in the morning. For now, you need to eat and sleep. We will talk tomorrow.'

'I don't want to talk to you.'

She felt her mouth curl, and then thought of camels and closed it again, but she knew she was still pouting.

'That's better.'

He gave her a tired smile, and she didn't understand why. Goodness, he looked dreadful. Still beautiful, but compared to the man she'd seen this morning he looked utterly drained. Shattered…

He glanced at the books that had been placed by her bed. 'You've got something to read. That's good.'

'Yes, it's as if I've been given a toy box to entertain me...' Her words faded. Violet knew her acrimony was misplaced. But the gesture was a painful reminder of her past.

He peered into the trunk. 'It looks like my mother's old school books.'

She said nothing.

'I won't disturb you again,' he told her. 'You have your privacy, I promise. I won't come in.' He was very direct. 'I can assure you nothing will happen here.'

'Oh...' Her voice was dark with warning. 'It had better not.'

'Violet, I am appalled at what has occurred. Tomorrow, if you're willing, I want to hear about it, so I can deal appropriately with my staff,' he said. 'I am not putting you on a helicopter with anyone who has mistreated you.'

Violet swallowed. She hadn't really been mistreated; the only thing that had been wounded was her heart.

'If you need me—'

'I won't need you.'

'You might hear—'

'I'm not scared of things that go bump in the night.'

She looked at him then—really looked. At his liquorice eyes, at his gorgeous tall frame, at the man she should perhaps hate, but didn't. Certainly hating him would be the safer alternative.

'I don't need anyone, Sahir,' Violet said, and picked up one of the books. 'I worked that out a long time ago.'

'I shall make that call and then come back. If you have any questions—'

'I won't.'

The bells signalled his leaving.

She was too weary to think about the day's events, and yet too wired to sleep.

She was also bored with her hunger strike—especially when such treats had been placed by her side.

The *gaz* was lovely, and the hot chocolate delicious—especially because he'd made it. It was sweet, but with a bitter edge, and so creamy that even after she'd finished it, even after she'd turned off the lamp, she could taste the sweet remnants on her lips as she lay there waiting for sleep.

She should be exhausted, surely?

But there was that prickly feeling that came from being alone in a new place, and it was a feeling that was all too familiar.

She made a quick dash for the loo, and attempted an even quicker dash back, because this tent was by far too big to be alone in, but on her way back she saw his softly lit room.

Poor Pria...

How Violet had shouted when she'd first seen it, and demanded a space of her own.

She stood at the entrance, feeling less terrified now he'd arrived.

Softly lit lamps illuminated the very masculine, sensual space. There the rugs weren't patterned, but thick and soft. Some looked like fur.

There was a lit fire with a huge dome above it—like a huge candle snuffer, should the heat get too much. And well it might, for she could feel the warmth even from where she stood.

Everything deserved to be explored, but her eyes were drawn to the vast bed. To call it a four-poster would be an injustice. There was an intricate patterned headboard that stretched right up to the dark wood ceiling—it really was like a room within a room. The heavy drapes were neatly tied back, and she wondered what it would be like to lie in that bed with them closed. They were of the same dark jade velvet of the cushion she'd sat on, and given how long she'd waited on it, Violet knew how soft they would feel.

Still, she walked over and ran her hand over one, then stroked the bedcover. The fabric was cool to the touch, while her body felt warm from the fire.

How could she still want him?

How could she want to climb in and close the drapes and wait for him to return?

Hide from the world with him?

No.

She went back to her own bed—in her far cooler, hastily made-up room—and lay looking at the ceiling, wishing it was last night, when she'd been in his arms with no idea of what was to come.

It had been the most peace she'd ever known…

The tent's roof really did move…and the one thing her first helicopter ride had taught her was that she really was in the middle of nowhere.

Oh, where was he?

Unable to sleep, she needed distraction, not to dwell on her plight, so she turned on the lamp and picked up a beautifully bound book.

Goodness, it belonged behind glass, Violet thought, or she should be wearing gloves. Because it was exquisite…

She opened the book slowly and looked at the carefully scripted name inside.

Anousheh.

Was that his mother's name?

It really was a gorgeous book, Violet thought. And it was beautifully illustrated.

She read a poem and didn't really get it. But then, while she might normally have skimmed over it, she saw a tiny scribbled note that helped.

Such need!

She looked at the words, which had been underlined, and read the poem again, with widening eyes.

Were Sahir here she might be tempted to tell him that she doubted this was one of his mother's old school books.

These poems were sensual…and so erotic.

Not all of them, but the Queen's underlining habit made it

easy to find the good parts, and Violet lay reading about buds and clamshells and such...

So engrossed was she, she barely glanced up when she heard the bells that signalled his return. But as he turned off the lamps in the living area she knew she should turn out her own.

Then she heard running water, and wondered if he was going to have a bath or a shower. She did her very best not to picture him naked, and hoped he'd be ages, because she wanted to read just one more poem.

Oh, my goodness!

She glanced up as his lamp went on, and of course she could hear him. Surely that was by design, for there should be strings being plucked and beauties reclining upon the cushions. Well, there would have been a hundred or so years ago.

Unfortunately, her bedtime reading had moved on from clamshells to 'tumescence', heavily underlined. It was like reading a diary, while at the same time not.

It was timeless pleasure that was being addressed here.

Placing the book face-down, she realised she could see the shadow of Sahir's member through the tent's wall. He was not erect, but he was certainly not flaccid, either, and she found that her hand had slipped from her shoulder and she was cupping her own breast.

She pulled it away, telling herself that he couldn't see her, and got back to the gorgeous poem.

And the next.

Had she been a little hasty in her warning to him that nothing could take place?

'Stop it...' she said aloud, trying to talk sense into herself, then closed the book and turned off her own lamp.

She heard a soft 'clank' and realised the dome must have been lowered over the fire in the next room as darkness fell.

Thankfully there were no more shadows to mire her mind...

CHAPTER EIGHT

DESPITE THE LATE NIGHT, still Sahir rose early.

Ah, but so too had Violet.

He returned from his morning horse ride to the sight of Violet seated on a low couch, wearing a pale silver robe with her blonde hair worn loose. She was sorting some books and folders into piles.

'You look...' His voice tapered off, her eyes flashing him a warning that his opinion was not required. 'I hope you slept well.'

Violet didn't respond; instead she concentrated on the books she'd retrieved from the trunk.

Sahir took a seat at the low table where Bedra had set up breakfast. Violet was blushing, furious with herself for noticing how stunning he looked in a black robe, unshaven, and thinking of the body beneath...how she had watched his shadow...

She was confused that she wanted him still.

'Come and eat,' he said.

'No, thank you.'

'Violet...'

That was all he said—but, yes, she was starving, and also she wanted to know what was happening, so she stood and made her way over.

'This bread is sweet.' He showed her the selection, clearly remembering her preferences. 'Do you want mint tea?'

'No.'

He raised two gorgeous black eyebrows at her lack of manners, but she refused to play nice. She glanced at his cheek. Of course she hadn't left so much as a mark.

Damn!

She peeled apart some of the bread and saw that there was a gorgeous gooey mix inside—dates, and nuts, and perhaps honey too—and, yes, it tasted delicious.

'Are you sure you don't want some tea?' He lifted the silver pot.

Too proud, again she shook her head. 'I prefer English Breakfast...'

'I'll ask Bedra if we have black tea.'

'Please don't,' Violet said, uncomfortable with the women's presence and wanting to talk to him alone. 'My tastes are very specific.'

'They weren't the other morning,' Sahir pointed out, slightly tongue in cheek.

'I liked you then,' Violet responded easily. 'I could forgive you for not having my exact choice.' She picked at the bread, and then filled the silence. 'Usually, I take them with me. My own teabags.'

'Really?'

She nodded.

'Take them where?'

'Work.' She glanced up. 'Or if I go away for a weekend or to a friend's.'

'I see.' He seemed to ponder that for a moment. 'You actually bring your own tea to work?'

'Yes.'

'Is it very expensive?'

'No.' She told him the brand. 'It's strong.'

'Well, this is delicate,' he told her. 'Baby mint leaves from the palace garden...spearmint leaves too. And I believe some green tea. And a little honey, from the palace bees… Perhaps not to your standards.'

'Fine…' She pushed forward a delicate glass and watched as the pale brew was poured. And, yes, it looked fresh, and gorgeous, and utterly perfect.

'Shame it doesn't come in teabags,' she said.

It was her first smile. Fleeting, but he felt a heady relief that it had returned to her features.

'Faisal is sorting out the dress,' he told her.

'I bet he can't get it back—'

'Violet,' he broke in. 'Consider it sorted.'

'Did you arrange my transport?'

'There is transport already scheduled in a few days.' He put down his glass. 'To use the phone for that would be…' He didn't know quite how to capture the word. '*Darar.* A disservice…misuse.'

'Of transport?'

'Of the desert,' he said. 'The line to the palace is for the most serious emergency.'

'Yet you sorted the dress.'

'Because you told me that was urgent. Time here is considered valuable. Exceptionally so.' He saw two straight lines form above her pretty nose. He smiled. 'If I call for…say, your teabags, yes, there is a temporary solution, but at a cost.'

'What cost?'

'You don't taste the fresh mint. More importantly, you don't speak. Or, if I am here alone, I don't get the space and the time to reflect.'

'But I should never have been brought here.'

'I agree, and I want to know all that has occurred.'

Violet frowned.

'I came back to find you gone,' he told her. 'Faisal was perturbed.'

'The butler?'

'Major-domo,' he corrected, but only so he could better explain. 'Faisal is the head of my household in London. He is distressed—as is Pria.'

'You had no right…'

'Violet.' He closed his eyes, about to remind her that this was not his doing, but she was his responsibility, and it was his own team that had done this, so he accepted her words. 'Can I speak?'

'No.'

'Explain?'

'No.' Violet refused to hear him. 'I want to go home.'

'As you wish. I shall make the call and we will never have to discuss this again. You can hate me for the rest of your life.'

'I don't hate,' she retorted, because that was an active choice she had made long ago. 'And I don't hate you.'

'Then why not listen?'

She looked up, and though she knew she ought to demand again to leave, so much of her wanted to stay…to at least understand what had occurred. Deep down, she knew that this was her only chance to have time with him, that if she left now she would have to live with so many unanswered questions.

She sat for a second, wanting to talk, but refusing to give in. Wanting to leave, while preferring to stay.

'I'm going for a walk,' she said at last.

'I'll come with you.'

'I don't need an escort.'

'Violet, you do. You should know there is wind, and there could be a sand storm.'

Bedra helped her strap on desert footwear and Violet was ticklish. Both women laughed.

All smiles faded, though, as she stepped with him into the desert. It was dazzling, and bright, and she was glad not to be out here alone—not that she'd admit that.

'It's like being a prisoner, walking with an escort.'

'Violet, this is not a prison,' he told her again. 'If you want to leave—'

She interrupted him, because that hadn't been what she meant. And she truly didn't know if she wanted to leave without hearing all he had to say.

'My father was in and out of prison when I was growing up,' she said, and then she paused, knowing from experience the next question people asked, so just answered it. 'Fighting, assault, theft, public disorder...' There was quite a list. 'I always had to have someone with me when I visited him. Even if we went for a walk.'

'Where was your mother?'

'Who knows?' Violet shrugged.

As she walked, she could feel his eyes on her, but he made no shocked comment—his silence was his only enquiry.

'She tended to run wild when my father was inside,' she told him. 'I'd generally be placed in foster care till he got out. Or if he partied too hard on his return.' She didn't quite know why she was telling him this, yet there was an odd sense of relief in telling him the truth. 'I'm sure the palace staff would be horrified at you sleeping with such riff-raff.'

'Violet, I did not say that and nor would I.' He asked a question. 'Where are they now?'

'I don't know,' she admitted.

'How long since you've seen them?'

'I got my own place at sixteen.' She shrugged. He could do the maths himself—it felt too awful to admit it had been nine years. 'There have been a couple of phone calls. Normally when they want money.' She shook her head. 'I don't want to talk about it. I was just saying that this reminds me of that— walking with a stranger.'

'I'm not a stranger.'

'You are to me.'

Even so, being out in the desert was far less daunting with

Sahir by her side—though she didn't really want to admit that. Actually, everything—from weddings with angry mothers of the bride to highbrow receptions and, yes, even sex—was far less daunting with Sahir.

'The desert abode is set so it cannot easily be seen. Good for enemies…not so much for English roses walking alone.'

'I'm hardly an English rose…'

'A violet.'

'More like an overheated tulip,' she said, and the return of his low laugh caught her by surprise.

She was starting to understand that his laughter was rare.

What they had found had been rare.

Yet it was all sullied now.

She followed him into the stables, but stood back as he checked on the animals.

'This is Noghré.'

Violet stood back as he patted the stallion he'd ridden this morning.

'Now, you have to see his foal.'

Violet followed him further into the stables, and closed her eyes at the shaded cool.

A stable hand let out a tiny foal. She was white, prancing, and she bounded to Violet with enthusiasm.

Violet took a step back.

'You can stroke her…'

'No, thank you.' She declined the nudges from the foal. 'I don't want to get fond of her.'

Wow, she knew how to guard that heart, Sahir thought, and it hollowed him out, thinking of the trust she'd placed in him the other night and how badly she'd been let down since then.

As the stable hand took the foal back to her pen he glanced over at Violet, still refusing to look at it, and he walked over to another stall and gave a low whistle.

The sweetest head popped out.

'Hey, Josie,' he said. 'You've been cheating on your diet, I hear.'

'Don't be mean,' Violet said as she went over.

Then she giggled when she looked in—because, yes, Josie was rather the exception to the muscled horses she'd seen so far.

Nervously, she patted her lovely nose. 'I've never stroked a horse before,' she said, and smiled, feeling the hot air from the mare's nostrils.

'She's gentle…nice to ride, if you want?'

'No, I'm fine stroking her. I always wanted a pet.'

'You've never kept an animal?'

'No.'

'What pet did you want?'

It was Violet who shook her head now.

She wasn't going to be telling him her thoughts and her hopes.

There was something, though, that Violet knew she should tell him…

Bedra prepared her a bath before dinner. Violet tried to help her with the jugs of water, but she shooed her away, telling her to sit down.

Violet couldn't, so she rinsed out her knickers and bra instead and felt so guilty. Everyone had been lovely. Well, apart from Aadil. But, given he'd told her that Sahir was to be married, perhaps it was a case of shooting the messenger?

She hadn't been mistreated. Not in the scheme of things. And she didn't want to get anyone into trouble.

'*Shukran,*' she said to Bedra. 'Bye.'

Violet waved—because, honestly, she knew otherwise she'd sit on the stool and watch, or offer to wash her hair.

The bath was bliss, and she lay with her eyes closed, listening to the wind, wishing she'd stroked that little foal, that she'd dared to say yes to riding Josie. Because even if she should be snarling and angry, in truth...

She stopped right there and hauled herself out of the bath, dashing across the lounge, while Sahir was in his quarters as Amal set up for dinner.

She thought the robe selection must have been left over from harem days, or everyone in the harem had been slender, because they all clung ridiculously.

As well as that, she'd just washed her only set of underwear.

She settled for a nice, safe pinkish beige robe, that had long sleeves. They were a bit tight and...too long.

Far too long.

She found that out at dinner, as they sat in candlelight and she tried to roll up her sleeves in case they dragged in the gorgeous food.

'Here.' He picked up her hand and took the hem of one sleeve, hooked it over her middle finger.

'Oh.' She let him do the other one, looking at her fingers peeking out of the silky fabric. 'I hope I don't ruin it.'

She was close to ruining *him*, Sahir thought. He had sworn nothing would happen, and then she'd walked out. And in candlelight the dress was the shade of nude flesh, outlining her hips, her waist and breasts.

Violet was determined to remain cross, but as they ate in silence she looked at the candelabras, the food and the goblets, and then she looked at the man opposite her.

She put down a very fat date and said what she knew she had to.

'Your staff were all kind. Well, there was one who was abrupt. But he was never rough or...'

'How did he get you onto the plane?'

'I was told there had been a security breach and that we needed to leave. I thought you were hurt or...' She took a shaky breath. 'Pria arrived as we were getting in the car. She seemed shocked. She was trying to call you, Faisal was too, but Aadil said it was on the King's orders.'

Sahir gave one nod.

'I thought you were on the plane.'

Violet had run up the steps, sure he would be there, but she didn't tell him that part!

'It took off. I went a bit crazy. It was then that Aadil told me to calm down. That he was trying to avoid a scandal because you were soon to marry.'

He closed his eyes, then opened them as she spoke on.

'Pria was lovely. She told me not to be scared, that you would sort it out.'

'What about the helicopter?'

'It was waiting at the palace. Like I said, no one was dreadful. I just don't get it.'

'I don't fully…' His voice was both serious and thoughtful. 'Your marriage age is thirty?'

Violet frowned.

'You said you hoped to marry by thirty. I was aiming to get to forty. I think things were being moved along.' He looked at her. 'And then you were seen on the balcony.'

'I'm hardly the first woman you've brought back home.'

'No, but after I left you, I demanded to take some time off. My father told me about an important meeting and I said my younger brother could step up. I don't usually. I just wanted…'

He met her eyes, and she could see the candlelight flickering in them, a dance of flames with dark corridors of desire behind them.

'Time,' he said.

'How much time?'

'A week.'

She swallowed, for his eyes told her that the week was to have been reserved for her.

'I was going to discuss spending the week with you. That has never happened before.'

He was clearly being honest.

'Oh.'

'I don't even know if you'd have wanted to spend more time with me.'

Violet averted her gaze because she had to. His eyes took her to a place where she was being made love to by him, and she refused to succumb, to nod, to say, *Yes, Sahir, I'd have wanted to spend a week with you.*

'A final fling before your marriage?' She took up her own goblet and drank the herby, syrupy brew.

'I've told you I didn't know it was about to happen.'

She swallowed, and saw his eyes were on her throat as she did so.

'Look, I don't expect you to understand, but here a marriage is not about love. Intimacy and conversation are separate.'

'How?'

'The King and Queen work together. For more trivial matters they can take a lover, or confidant.'

'Trivial?' Violet checked.

'These are the laws—country first, everything else second.'

'And you agree?'

'I don't make the rules. I'm not saying they have to take a lover. Just that they can.'

'I don't get it,' Violet said again.

'Of course you don't. You're not going to be a king or a queen.'

'I meant…' She could feel her skin hot under her robe. 'I mean, presumably there would have to be heirs.'

'Of course.'

'So how?' She looked at him. 'How would they…?'

'It's sex, Violet, it doesn't have to be about love.'

'So, in this strictly business marriage, do they meet once a month, or…?'

'The teller states when the time is right for an heir and then they come here.'

'Oh.' She blinked. 'So, this "teller" decides the stars have aligned and off to the desert they go?'

'It sounds clinical, but...'

'No,' Violet refuted. 'It sounds rather lovely. Well, the stars aligning and the coming to the desert part does. It's the long, lonely stretches in between that would get to me. I doubt I'd be in the mood if my husband was off taking care of *"trivial"* matters with someone else.' She shrugged. 'But what would I know?'

Sahir breathed through his nostrils.

Violet knew how to press certain buttons, how to voice the questions he asked himself at times, and yet she did it with a smile, in a vaguely dizzy voice, when she was anything but.

'As I said, taking a lover is an option.'

He took a cleansing breath, watched as she helped herself to more dessert. Of course she could never understand. It felt important, though, to explain to her what had occurred.

'I didn't know anything until I returned to the house and you were gone,' he told her. 'I first thought you had been taken to the palace. Emotion is something we don't allow, but I spoke angrily with my father.'

'The King?'

Sahir nodded.

'Don't you get on?'

'We are not close, but we're not enemies. I have my own office, my team. I'm perplexed. I still cannot believe he sanctioned it. He seemed to think he was doing us a favour by giving us some discreet time.'

'What did you say when you spoke to him?'

'I told him to stay the hell out of my business.'

'And what did he say?'

'That the welfare of the country is my only business.'

* * *

Violet didn't ask to be excused. Just removed herself from the table and went over to the trunk she'd dragged into the lounge area.

As her thoughts whirred she went through it.

She could see things from Sahir's point of view a little more. Not just from what he'd said, but because she remembered the grey tinge to his complexion when he'd arrived last night. The relief in his eyes when he'd first seen her.

He came and lay on the sofa, staring at the roof of the tent as if still trying to work things out.

It was a nice silence. Not the tense one of before. Just a little pause as she sorted the books into piles and the wind sounded like music in the distance.

She rummaged in the trunk, looking at all the papers and treasures.

'Bedra didn't mean to offend you by bringing you that.' He glanced over. 'I think she was just trying to help.'

'I know. It just felt like…' She looked over to the one person she was really able to turn off her fake smile for and decided to tell him why it had upset her so. 'I was placed in a lot of foster homes…'

'So you had a lot of toy boxes?'

She nodded and ran her hand over the ancient gleaming wood. 'Sometimes there would be a jigsaw…'

'Missing parts?'

'No time to finish it. Or I'd find something I liked and then it would be time to go and I'd have to leave it behind. It wasn't always the case. Things calmed down somewhat as I got older. And I spent a lot of time with Grace and her mother.'

'It must have hurt when Mrs Andrews accused you.'

'I'm very used to it.' She made light of the painful topic, but then caught his serious, patient eyes. 'I was mortified,' she admitted, and felt her throat tighten even as she spoke. 'I die on the inside whenever things go missing.'

'Why?'

'I'm terrified people will think it's me.'

'Mrs Andrews was clearly confused.'

Violet nodded. She could hear the wind howling outside and she felt so removed from the world. And, despite her situation, she simply felt free not to lie.

'It was Grace questioning me that really hurt.' She had never said that—not even to Grace. 'I don't blame her. I get that it was easier for her to think I'd taken something rather than that her mother was so ill. She's always trying to talk about it now, or say sorry.'

'You're still too angry to hear it?'

'Oh, no.' She shook her head. 'I was never angry—just terrified I was going to lose her friendship.'

'Violet…'

'Don't.'

She put up her hand and then went back to the trunk, grateful for the distraction.

Her heart came to a stop when she saw a photo of the late Queen Elizabeth II with… 'Oh, goodness.' Her emotions changed like the wind. 'I thought this was you.'

'Show me?'

'Is this in London?'

'Yes.' Sahir propped himself onto one elbow to look. 'That's my father.'

'He looks about twelve.'

'He'd have been about eighteen…' He took a moment, as if to work out the year it had been taken. 'No, he'd have been nineteen.'

'Where's your mother?'

'This was before they were married. It was his first solo tour. What else is in there?' he asked.

'Menus,' Violet said delightedly. 'Maybe they'll give me some ideas. At work, we all bring in something to eat on a Friday… Oh, well, I guess I won't be needing these…'

'You're going to miss working a lot?'

'Yes,' Violet admitted, flicking through the cards. 'But maybe it's the change I need. I mean I always—and I mean always—wanted to be a librarian. I was also keen to study, but I didn't want to move away.'

'How come?' he probed. 'Why are you so reluctant to move away?'

She paused in flicking through the menu cards and met his gaze. She liked how he didn't react when she told him things, how his expression didn't change and he didn't judge. Sahir's calm made her feel able to admit something she never had before.

'I don't want to leave in case my parents ever decide to look me up.'

He nodded.

'They wouldn't be able to find me.'

He said nothing. Yes, she liked his calm…how he didn't react.

Inwardly Sahir did react.

I would find you, he wanted to say, but knew those words could only hurt.

She had put her career, her future, on hold, in the hope that one day her parents might look her up, or drop in.

He felt a real sadness. One he'd been taught not to feel, let alone reveal.

He felt everything now. Since Violet had appeared in his life he felt the world more intensely, and he breathed through the wave of anger that seemed to crush him for a moment as Violet got back to the menu cards.

'Ooh, what's Persian Love Cake?'

'Cake,' he responded gruffly. His voice betrayed him, so he corrected it and elaborated. 'With petals on. Tastes of rose water…'

'I'm going to make it,' Violet said. 'Once I've been freed.'

He took a deep breath.

'Kidding!' She looked over and gave him a small smile.

'Good.'

He stared at the tent roof as she went through all the menus and he realised he'd been right the first time—she did recover quickly.

The hurt was still there, though.

'You could get a job anywhere,' he said, in as even a tone as he could summon.

'Oh, please… I have no qualifications, no experience apart from at the library. And please don't offer to help,' she warned. 'I'd hate that.'

'Then I won't—and anyway, you don't need my help. You have a lot going for you.' He looked at her. 'You must be reliable, if you've worked there for so long. Loyal…'

She was many, many things, he thought.

'Maybe it's time to think about what you really want.'

'I'd like this.' Again, she changed the subject and held up another menu card. 'Christmas dinner at the Savoy. I'd love to go there.'

'I'm being serious.'

'So am I,' she said.

But she would not look up, and he knew she was hurting, and he loathed it that he did not know how to fix this, that she refused his help.

He sensed she did not want to discuss it further. 'What's on the menu?' he asked.

'Turkey,' she read. 'Sole.'

He smiled when she pulled a face at the thought of fish.

'Skip to the dessert, Violet,' he said. 'You know you want to.'

'Actually, no!'

She laughed, about to tell him she loathed fruit cake, but then she saw all the ticks beside a few of the dishes—neat little ticks that she recognised from the Queen's markings on the books.

'This is…' She was about to tell him, but then, turning the menu over, she abruptly stopped.

It was dated.

'What?' he asked.

Violet was silent, frantically doing the maths in her head.

'What?' he asked again, and she looked up, her face flushed.

'I was going to say it's less expensive than I thought it would be, but it's an old menu.'

It was from the Christmas before Sahir had been born.

Violet said nothing more, but went through the trunk with a keener interest now.

There were some gorgeous jewels contained in a little pouch. She poured them into her hand. 'Are these real?'

He barely glanced over.

'I would think so,' he said. 'We don't have any…'

'Costume jewellery?' She rolled her eyes. 'You are such a snob.'

She looked at the gorgeous sapphires, diamonds and rubies, all just exquisite, and then carefully replaced them in the pouch.

'Here's a report card…' she said. Then she read the name. 'It's your father's.'

'We went to the same school.' He rolled his eyes.

She read through it. 'It says that he's kind and thoughtful.'

'So long as he gets his own way. I think they probably only said such nice things because of his title.'

'Did they say nice things about you?'

'They did,' he agreed. 'Because I was an excellent student.'

'Arrogant?'

'"Confident", I believe they said…'

'Did you like boarding school?'

'I would have liked it a lot better without Aadil guarding me.'

'You really don't like him?'

'No. He was always snooping…reporting back to my father. He was the one who told me that my mother had died.'

'What did he tell you?' Violet asked.

'The truth.'

Violet frowned.

'He told me she was ill. That it was serious, and I was needed back home. I wanted to see her. He took a message after we boarded the jet and then started going through protocol.'

'Protocol?'

'For if the Queen dies, or the King, or whoever…'

Violet nodded, trying to imagine what that must be like—to be losing someone you love and having to think of protocol.

'I told him that I was aware of my role and that it was offensive of him to speak like that when she was fighting for her life…'

Violet nodded. 'I'd have felt the same.'

'Well, he barely glanced up from his papers, then he said, "The Queen has already died."'

Violet gasped. 'That's how he told you?'

'He then added "Your Highness", and offered his condolences, but, yes, that was how he told me.' He looked over. 'I think he was trying to provoke me.'

'Provoke?'

'He was hoping for a reaction. I think he thought it would be better for me to be upset at thirty thousand feet rather than on landing. I've told you—a royal cannot show emotion. It unsettles the people.'

'I think having a cold and unfeeling ruler would be more unsettling,' Violet said. 'At least that's how it would seem to me.'

'The people need to know their rulers won't fall apart in a crisis. I used to question it, but after my mother died…'

She stared at him, trying to demand with her eyes that he be honest—for she had been, after all.

* * *

'It was a turbulent time for our country,' Sahir said. 'My father had to work hard, make decisions that would impact the nation's future, and he did so unfailingly. I took a month out of school but I barely saw him. He was up at dawn, and would take morning briefings from Aadil in the gardens. I almost failed that year at school. Sometimes I would forget to eat…'

He was silent, remembering it.

'I managed all my royal duties, but only just. I knew if I got upset then Ibrahim and Jasmine would follow suit. I had to put aside my own guilt.'

He regretted his words immediately, because of course she pounced.

'Guilt?'

He stood up, ending the conversation. 'I believe most people feel that way when they lose someone.'

'But you're the Crown Prince,' Violet said. 'You don't get to feel.'

His back stiffened. 'No.' He turned around. 'And I don't get to share.' He nodded. 'Goodnight.'

'Stay.' She sat still, holding another book. 'Talk.'

'No.' He shook his head. 'Better not.'

He went to his rooms, shut off the fire, stripped and climbed into bed.

He watched the lounge darken.

Then saw Violet's shadow on the wall.

Politely he closed his eyes as she undressed, for she had clearly not worked out how erotic this space could be.

He opened them again and thankfully saw she was in bed. He could see her reading, her hair still up, and then he watched her turn her head to one side, picking up the howl of a lone Arabian wolf. She got back to reading.

Violet really was inquisitive rather than fearless.

And very sensible to have cut that silken cord.

How he ached to reach for it now…

* * *

The wind was soft, like a little whistle or a howl, and yet it was so still in here.

She paused in her reading and heard another wolf howling—or was it two, or three?

The poor Queen, Violet thought, stuck in her businesslike marriage. Because from all she'd read Anousheh hadn't just adored the sensual poets, but the romantic ones too.

She read a poem about ageing love and silver hair, and found there were tears in her eyes... Only she wasn't sure if they were for Queen Anousheh or for herself.

She wanted Sahir—more of Sahir—and yet she had warned him in no uncertain terms to stay back.

And she wanted to go riding, to play with the little foal and just explore this incredible place...

Then be sent away.

She got back to the sensual poems, reaching for a drink of water. But the glass was empty and she couldn't be bothered to fill it.

She saw her own shadow on the wall, and then looked up and saw she was there on the ceiling too, her hand outstretched for the glass.

Her fingers were far longer than they were in real life...even the curls at the ends of her hair were magnified and somehow enhanced. Her eyes were heavy with sleep, and she thought she could even see her eyelashes flutter...

It was hypnotic...lying there, watching herself...

Her shadow self.

Or was it the real her?

Violet didn't know. And even though she got back to her book her shadow was still there, and apparently braver than she...more accepting of the low throb of desire in her stomach... The woman who danced across the walls as she lifted her leg and looked at her toes didn't mind where she was, or the circumstances that had brought her here.

Goodness, those poems made her bold—or was it something about the desert that lured her other side out? Was it simply that the man who had brought her here made her feel she could be whoever she really was?

Whoever she wanted to be?

Violet climbed out of the low bed and stood still. Oh, she was not *that* bold. She wasn't about to follow her shadow where it tempted her to go. No, she would not be slipping into Sahir's bed. Nor was she about to perform for him…

In the scheme of things, it could be considered tame. All she did was stand and lift the heavy jug by her bed, fill her goblet with water.

She did not glance up to check her shadow, nor did she intend to taunt.

Perhaps a little.

She took out the combs from her hair. Really, she only did what she might do at home…

It just felt very different here.

Sahir lay there.

He did not politely avert his gaze from her erect nipples…

He enjoyed the slow shake of her head as she loosened her hair and then climbed slowly into bed…

He knew that was for him.

Of course Violet would have worked it out.

And now she was taunting him for being the first to say goodnight.

When possibly she should be grateful that he wouldn't make her his lover tonight.

She could never be Queen.

A lover, a confidant—whatever the way it was described— that was all she could ever be for him.

Sahir knew one thing, and it kept him from turning on the lamp, beckoning her to his bed.

She deserved more.

CHAPTER NINE

VIOLET WOKE TO no shadows.

She lay there, staring and still a little more bold, more curious... And, no, she would not hide, or sulk, or even justify why she'd climbed out of bed last night as she heard him pass.

'Sahir...?'

He was just on his way out when she appeared, holding the curtain over her scant nightwear.

'Good morning, Violet.'

Her cheeks were red, and they stared at each other for a moment, both aware that last night he'd seen what lay behind the curtain.

'Can I come with you?' she asked.

'I'm going riding.'

'I know you are.' Violet nodded. 'I've decided I'd like to try.'

'You've never ridden?'

'I want to try new things, and you said Josie was a good horse to learn on.'

'I'll have the stable manager—'

'No,' Violet said. 'I don't want to go riding with someone I don't know.' Her eyes met his. 'When do we leave here?'

'Tomorrow night.'

'Then I might never get this chance again.'

'Very well. But a short lesson, or you'll be in agony.'

He stood outside the curtain as she pulled off her nightgown.

'What do I wear?' she asked.

'Just a robe. I shall sort out some chaps.'

'Chaps?' she asked from behind the screen, doing up the tiny buttons down the front of a lilac gown. 'What are they?'

'Leg coverings made of leather.'

'Sahir!' she chided in a voice she had never known she owned. 'We barely know each other!'

And he let her flirt, let her be free, and even if she didn't appreciate the way she'd arrived, oh, she knew she did not want to leave the desert.

Or him.

At the stables, he handed her the most awful-looking things. 'What on earth…?'

'You need to wear them,' he said, watching as she attempted to put the chaps on. 'The other way.'

'Can you at least help?' she asked, although she never usually did.

He glared but, ever polite, took the chaps and knelt.

And now he was being all gentlemanly, even as she lifted her robe, barely touching her as he buckled the straps.

As good as his word.

Aagh!

'Stay still…' he warned.

'I'm trying,' Violet said, feeling a touch deflated because he showed no reaction.

He seemed irritated, in fact.

'You're not a very nice teacher,' she said, when he snapped at her fourth attempt to mount a very placid Josie.

'Because I'm not a teacher,' he said. 'I offered the best horseman in Janana to give you a lesson. But, oh, no…'

'You're not very patient.'

'And you're not very good at listening.'

'I've never been so close to a dog, let alone a horse.'

He felt his heart crack as he thought of all the horses he had, the cats and the dogs, and the birds that tapped on the palace windows.

Then he thought of her not stroking the little foal, and how fiercely she guarded her heart. He could feel she was trusting him, knew she was flirting, and it felt like a gift.

He wanted that gift, and yet what did he offer in return?

'Can you move that stool?' she asked.

'It's called a mounting block,' he corrected. 'And it's where it should be.'

She stood up, trying it all over again.

'Balance your weight,' he told her.

'I am,' she said. 'It's the getting my leg…'

Josie really was rather large, and he saw Violet just couldn't stretch her leg far enough, so ended up lying prone over the saddle.

'Violet!' he snapped—but not in a terse way. It was more like the noise the velvet rope had made as it slithered over her head.

And then the tension gave, and he laughed. Not the mirthless shouts of laughter he occasionally gave, nor even the softer, shorter bursts. This was a low, deep laugh that he released as she lay there, face down. He even playfully slapped her bottom, and she almost cried with laughter as he prised her leg up and over and practically hauled her into position.

'I'm upright!'

Josie moved a couple of steps and she squeaked.

'Do I need a riding hat?'

'You do not.' He walked Josie around for a few moments. 'Look ahead,' he told her. 'You don't look down when you drive.'

'I can't drive,' she informed him. 'There's no need in London. Anyway, I have no sense of direction.' She smiled down at him. 'How am I doing?'

'Better,' he conceded.

'Can I trot?'

'Not yet.'

'Can I trot now?' she asked, all of six minutes later.

'Go on, then.' He nodded, confident in Josie, then frowned

in bemusement as Violet made some clicking noises. 'Give her a few squeezes with your legs.'

She seemed reluctant to, and even Josie gave him a confused glance. He spoke in Arabic to the old girl.

'What are you saying to her?' asked Violet.

'That you are very confident for someone so clueless.'

He gave Josie a tap and Violet let out a shriek as the horse sped off, Violet jolting up and down as she fought to stay on.

'How do I make her stop?' she yelled.

'Pull on the reins.'

'It worked!' Josie slowed to a walk and Violet, breathless and exhilarated, looked as if she felt she ruled the equestrian world. 'Can we go for a ride in the desert?'

'No.'

'I could do this at the local riding school at home.'

'You could—yet you never have,' he pointed out. 'You can't learn it all in one day. You're going to be sore.'

'I. Don't. Care,' Violet told him. 'I want a desert ride. It *is* my holiday, Sahir.'

'Holiday?'

'Well, it sort of is,' she said. 'And I don't want to waste it.' She gave him a smile. 'I've decided to embrace the time I have rather than endure it.'

And she was the most persuasive, guilt-inducing, incredible person he had ever met, because a short while later they were actually setting off, his beast chomping at the bit as Josie plodded along.

'How is it?' he asked as they left the tent far behind.

'So nice.' She closed her eyes. 'If I hadn't been kidnapped to get here, then this would be the best day of my life,' she teased.

He smiled, but it faded as his horse started to get stroppy. 'I'm going to stretch him—do you want to get off for a while?'

'No.'

'Violet…'

'I'll just keep walking.'

'But you won't…'

He felt it then—flashes of her deciding to trot, or gallop, or falling off…fears he did not allow himself to have.

And yet he'd been having them since the moment they'd met.

He kicked his horse, trying to outrun his thoughts, trying to rid his head of that moment when he hadn't cared what happened with King Abdul, or if he might be missed for a week.

And his head hadn't quite cleared even as he slowed and turned—for there she was, plodding along on Josie, her cheeks bright red and a smile on her face. He slowed his horse to a walk.

'We'll go back,' he told her.

'Not yet.' She looked at the endless dunes, and then she looked up to the sun. 'How do you find your way back?'

He told her about the observatory, how they were all taught about the stars…

'What if it's cloudy?'

'You'd know north.'

'No.'

'You'd know it.'

'I don't.' She shook her head. 'I must have missed that lesson. I'm not the brightest…'

'Violet.' He stopped her. 'You are one of the cleverest people I know.'

'I'm really not.'

'Oh, you are. We are all taught about the skies here, and the patterns of the land, the winds. It is just something I took for granted. The palace is built in the shape of a star…'

'I saw,' she said. 'Well, I noticed when the helicopter took off.'

'Were you terrified?'

'A bit.' She nodded as they rode on. 'But not adequately terrified.'

'What does that mean?'

'Just…given my situation, I wasn't that scared.'

As they rode he told her about the palace ruins his mother had loved.

'My father is adamant that they remain untouched. Or rather...' Sahir paused, for he did not discuss his thoughts with anyone, and yet he found that constantly challenged when he was with Violet.

He glanced over at her, saw the dreamy look in her eyes. She glanced back, as if expecting him to carry on speaking.

'The plans have to get passed by the council, and some of them are opposed.'

'But not all of them?'

'No.' He nodded. 'Unfortunately, it is the vocal few who are against change.'

'It always is.' She told him about the library committee. 'Honestly, it took for ever to get them to agree even to join social media.'

He smiled. 'We have the raw materials; the Bedouins have the skills.'

'They do for now.'

He frowned, unsure how Violet could speak so knowledgeably, but she turned and smiled.

'Use it or lose it.'

He laughed. 'I'll put that to the council.'

It was an incredible trip, and as they turned to head back, even though she'd been warned not to, Violet wasn't scared to persist with him.

'Can I ask a question?' Violet said. 'Just one.'

'One.'

'Why do you feel guilty about your mother?'

'Maybe because she was lonely, and unhappy.'

She knew when he was being evasive. And something told her that she was getting the standard Sahir reply.

'Don't bother answering if you're just going to fob me off,' she said.

* * *

'You really don't miss anything,' he said.

But then he paused, unsure whether or not to proceed. Yet she'd somehow trusted him, and now he felt the same way. It was something he had never shared before, though.

'She was breathless on our last walk,' he said. He had re-played that morning so many times. 'I should have noticed.'

'I'm out of breath now.'

'We've been out for two hours.' He gave her a slight smile, knowing she was trying to assuage his guilt, but it would never leave him.

They kept riding, the tent now in sight.

'She had a nosebleed. I caused it. I was scolding her...' He gave a pale smile at Violet's shocked expression. 'No, I did not hit my mother.'

'I know that, but...' She shook her head. 'What do you mean, you caused it?'

'My brother and sister had worked out that she had a confidant.'

He saw Violet holding in a gasp, trying to be as calm as he had been for her when she'd revealed her truth.

'I had always known. Aadil seemed to know too. He was my protection officer then, but his father was an elder on the council.' He glanced over, aware he probably wasn't making much sense, but Violet nodded.

'So, a bit of a stickler for the rules?'

'Correct.' He gave her a half-smile. 'As I've told you, there is a lot of leeway, but discretion is the absolute rule.'

'And she wasn't being discreet?'

'No. I was very concerned that she was going to get in trouble. And so I told her off. I told her to be more careful.'

'What did she say?'

'She started to laugh.'

They were almost back, and Sahir found he didn't want to be.

'Mother thought it was hilarious. She told me I was staid, and like my father, but then she was kind. She was always a bit wild, but she said she would be more careful, told me not to worry... And then her nose started bleeding.'

They were so close to the stables, to other people, and the horses seemed to intuit that, for they stopped.

'She had leukaemia.'

'You couldn't have known.'

He said nothing.

'Sahir?' She questioned his self-imposed silence with his name. 'Were there other signs?'

'I believe my father had noticed a bruise on her back, another on her thigh. She told him she had been exploring the ruins...'

'And did he rush her to the palace doctor?'

'No.' His voice was black. 'He did not. I was told she fainted at breakfast.'

He saw her look over at him.

'The doctor knew immediately that she was gravely ill. She was taken to the royal hospital. I was called out of school. It was that fast.'

'That's so sad... What was your father like afterwards?'

'Much the same as he'd always been. He said the country had lost a brilliant queen.'

'What else?'

'Truly? Not much. He went straight back to work—not that he had a choice. The country was on the edge of war.'

'Here?'

He nodded. 'My father was taking breakfast meetings with aides the morning after her funeral. I know he had to be, but he should have made time for Jasmine, at least.'

'What about Ibrahim?'

'He wanted to go back to school pretty much straight after.'

'And you?'

'I was back by October. There were some formalities for me

to attend to. After that, life just carried on. He barely mentions her now. I sometimes wonder if he misses her at all.'

The conversation was over. She knew that both from his curt tone and also because the stable hand was approaching.

She wished they had longer.

Even their whole week. Because it felt all too soon for their time to be over.

'Slowly…'

He guided her down and she felt her feet hit the ground. As she headed for the tent she saw a look pass between Sahir and the stable hand as she rather gingerly walked away.

'I warned you,' said Sahir.

'You did,' Violet said. 'I'm just a bit stiff…'

So was Sahir.

Back to being formal.

Even as she sank into the bath Bedra had prepared, Violet was naïve about the agony to come. Even as she sat and ate dinner, and tried to get comfortable on the floor, she had no idea what awaited her.

CHAPTER TEN

THEIR LAST MORNING and she didn't want it to be. Even before her eyes had opened she was dreading this day.

And then all her sorrows were dimmed by a new agony.

From her neck to her toes, Violet ached.

More than ached.

Somehow, she made it to the loo—and there was fresh agony there. It felt as if she was burning…

'Okay?' asked Sahir as she hobbled out, and there was nothing worse than feeling dreadful and being met by the sight of Sahir's toned body, naked apart from a black towel tied around his hips, on his way to bathe.

'I can barely move…'

'I warned you,' he said. 'I'll prepare you a bath.'

'Where's Bedra?'

'Morning prayers, probably,' he said. 'Do you want a bath or not?'

She nodded, and just had to stand as he poured jug after jug of water into the beautiful stone bath, with far more speed than Bedra. Like some doctor, he peered at various bottles and added oils and gorgeous scents, then bent over and beat at the water with his hand.

'It's quite warm…'

'I'm sure it will be perfect.' She forced a smile. 'Thank you.'

'You want me to leave?'

'Of course.'

'So you're going to get over the bath edge with the same dexterity you showed on the horse yesterday?'

He managed to sound practical even as he dripped sarcasm—enough so that she was cross enough not to blush as he helped her off with her nightgown.

'I'm so sore…'

'I know that you are,' he said. 'Check the temperature.'

She dipped her hand in and the water felt divine.

There was just one problem. Violet was so sore that she honestly wondered if she *could* get her leg over the edge, even with his help.

Sahir did not even attempt to solve that mystery. He just scooped her up and lowered her, bottom first, into the bath, trying not to remember when they'd bathed together. He recalled her protestations of discomfort that time…when she'd been sore for very different reasons.

'It's not funny,' she said, as he sat on the edge and pondered for a while.

'I'm not saying a word.'

He was watching her, wondering how it was possible to be this close to another person and to care this much, and yet also be a bit cross with them too, and annoyed with himself.

'It was foolish,' he said.

'Very,' Violet agreed. 'And now I can't move.'

More than that, nor could he move his heart. And he could not close it.

Foolish, indeed.

After he'd let her luxuriate in the warm water for a while he picked her up and carried her to the entrance to her own chamber. He lowered her down.

'You'll feel better soon—just move around.'

He gave his best advice and left, but then heard her moans as she tried to put her knickers on.

'Violet?' He called out to warn her that he was there. 'Can I come in?'

'Yes.'

'Where does it hurt?' he asked.

She was about to say *everywhere*, but the bath had in fact helped.

'My back…my thighs…'

'Where else?'

'My bottom.' She wasn't going to tell him about the bits in between. 'I had no idea. We only walked the horses.'

'Do you want a massage?'

'I'm not going to fall for that,' she shot back.

'Violet, I am offering to help with your pain, not to bed you.'

'*Bed* me…' she huffed. 'I should have known you were from the Dark Ages when you said that.'

'Do you want me to sort out your pain?'

'Yes.'

'We'll go to my room.'

'What's wrong with here?'

'Have you ever had a sports massage?'

'No.'

'It's far from sensual—and, believe me, I would fall off that little bed.'

He was so tall and wide she believed him.

'Fine,' she said.

And then she was being carried into his bedchamber, although on less sensual terms than she'd hoped. Certainly the poems she'd read hadn't prepared her for this.

He lowered her onto his bed and it was like falling into a cloud and being caught by angels.

'Your bed…' She sighed, but then her eyes narrowed. 'Shouldn't I be on a firm surface?'

'If you prefer, we can go on the floor—though I have found my bed has always sufficed.'

She felt jealous, wondering how many beauties had massaged his aches away right here, and wondering even more so as he reached to the bedside table and poured some oil into a dish.

'Is that your sex oil?'

'It's just oil,' Sahir corrected, taking off her towel, and instructing her to roll onto her stomach.

She was relieved that she had managed to get her knickers on.

'I've told you. I come here only to reflect.'

Violet wanted to verify if that meant he'd never brought a lover here. If that meant she was the first woman in this bed. But she decided it wasn't the time to ask.

He was being very formal.

Very much the Sahir she had first met.

'It might hurt a bit,' he told her.

'Okay.'

He started low on her neck and shoulders and it was far from sensual. His hands were almost rough as they worked on the knots. Then deftly he worked on her torso, and either side of her spine. Then he focussed on her tailbone for what seemed like for ever.

'Ow!'

'I know…'

Sahir closed his eyes, took a breath and found he was very grateful for his teachings—because he knew when he opened his eyes his voice would be stern as he told her to turn, and he was confident his features would be impassive.

She was slippery and warm as he turned her, and then his oiled hands came to her calves and her inner thighs, and he tried not to look at her breasts.

He even lifted her leg, like a physiotherapist, bending it at the knee and then doing the same with the other.

'Your hips are tight,' he said.

'Yes.'

He again refused to look at her breasts, or at her soft stomach, or even to focus too much on her face. Her eyes were tightly closed, and she gave just the occasional grimace, but then he felt her hips loosen and saw her slight smile.

'Better?'

'Somewhat...'

At least she was moving her legs now, and her back looked less stiff, though he knew she would not be telling him that she'd just found out what 'saddle sore' really meant.

Sahir knew, of course. And knew she must be in agony. But he would not be offering to sort that out. It was just nice to see her more relaxed.

'Walk around,' Sahir suggested. 'Loosen up.'

'I feel loose,' she said.

Too loose and limp to move. Though she made a half-hearted attempt to put her arm over her breasts, but then gave in and let it fall by her side.

'I don't want to move.'

'Then don't,' Sahir said. 'But I won't be offering to move you to the lounge.'

She gave a half-laugh at the very notion and he lay down beside her.

'You might get a couple of bruises; your shoulders were very tight.'

'I'll forgive you,' she said, feeling all floaty from his hands, and perhaps too relaxed to be subtle as her mind flitted like a lazy butterfly to the next topic. 'If your parents slept apart, how did your father notice your mother's bruises?'

'Perhaps they had the occasional...' He nudged her. 'Please don't make me think about that.'

She laughed a little, then they both fell quiet.

Soon it would be time for goodbye.

'What time do we leave?' she asked.

'Sunset.'

They lay listening to the wind, and she could feel her eyes getting heavy. She loved nothing more than the thought of dozing in his arms.

'We've never actually slept together,' she said, and smiled.

'We're sleep virgins,' Sahir said.

Then together they laughed at his little joke and it seemed to startle them both.

They turned their faces to each other.

'Sahir...' she grumbled, and he saw her pretty lips pouting.

That gesture had always annoyed him in the past. Seriously. Usually he did not like sulking or pouting. And yet with Violet it felt more like a code...a secret only he knew. Or was it the subtle shift in tone that alerted him to more than her pretty mouth?

'I'm so sore,' she said.

'I know.'

'I don't think you know where...'

'I said nothing would happen.'

'Please take it back.'

And it would have taken a will greater than any Sahir possessed not to lower his head and briefly kiss her.

The kiss was light, and yet she felt its soft weight. And although he did not linger, the contact lasted a second too long to be considered brief. There was just enough weight to his mouth that when he removed it she felt the little buzz of contact remain, and his kiss had allowed enough time to deliver its sensual intent.

His head hovered above hers and she stared into his eyes, trying to work out if they were a deep brown or a dark navy or were they both? Like a deep ocean that changed with each view.

His chest was above her own, not touching, but his hip was over hers and she wanted to arch, to feel the hair of his chest and the warmth of his skin. She longed for Sahir to kiss her again, but he just hovered, and waited, and looked down at her mouth.

She was not a petulant person—or she hoped she wasn't—and she never complained. But there was a new Violet that Sahir allowed to emerge when she was this close to him.

'I'm very sore,' she reiterated. 'In a place I'd rather not say.'

'Poor Violet,' he said, and gave her a sad smile.

She blinked, as if there were real tears in her eyes.

'Can I help in any way?' he asked.

'I don't know...' She sighed bravely, gallantly. 'I'm sure I'll be okay...'

His eyes swept down her pink chest and his hand lightly brushed one breast as it moved to her stomach. Then his gaze returned to her face and met hers completely as that hand moved down to stroke the blonde hairs peeking from the top of her knickers.

'Is it sore here?'

'Not quite,' she admitted. 'But you're close.'

'I see...'

He was very serious, moving her aching thighs apart just a little—though she might have helped with that—and then he cupped her through her knickers, his hand warm and gentle, but really quite firm. It really was rather lovely.

'How's that?' he asked, his voice gravelly.

'A bit better.'

'Why don't I take a proper look?'

He slipped off her knickers and oiled his hand, and she almost cried out as he touched her swollen and tender body.

'It will go.'

He stroked her inner thighs again, and then he cupped her—and, gosh, she hadn't known how nice it was to feel the soft oil and his touch.

'Distraction might help,' he said, and now he kissed her, softly still, but not briefly, and her hands moved into his raven hair.

And he really was the most excellent distraction, for she was pulling him closer, encouraging him to move over her. And now she felt the bliss of his chest, and then he knelt, and she felt so fluid.

He moved her down the silk sheet and carefully took her. 'Does it hurt?'

She did not know how to respond; she was sore, and swollen, but deep inside she was soaring.

'Oh, please...'

She stared at his face as he looked down, as he refused to give her what she needed—what their bodies demanded, but what she would certainly regret.

For Sahir, the restraint was more than erotic. Here in the desert he was taken by her pleasure. Captivated, he watched her, and there was almost a physical shift within her. He did not change his slow, deep rhythm. Something important was building... something impossible to contain.

'Violet...'

His voice summoned her from a dreamy delirium and she saw something new, something that told her the world as she knew it had changed...

She inhaled sharply, bit her bottom lip, and then she just stared back as he took her slowly, precisely...

She felt just the slightest feather touch of him against her sore vulva, over and over as he moved deep inside. Even the increasing speed of his thrusts, the deepening intensity that brought little pinches of tension to her thighs, that had her sex tightening, her back arching, were almost secondary to the feel of her heart opening to him.

The game had stopped, and she put her arm over her eyes because she knew now that she loved him.

'Help me,' she said.

Because she did not want it to be true, and she did not want it to end.

And then she really was helpless, just a writhe of knots and this orgasm that would almost hurt if he did not hold her steady—that would be agony if he did not spill into her with the same precision and slight distance with which he'd taken her.

'I can't—' she choked, feeling him pulse inside her, trying to tell herself she could not love this man when soon it would be time to say goodbye.

'I know.'

She pulled back her arm as he carefully pulled out. She wasn't sore—or possibly she was, but this deep revelation was certainly a distraction.

'Better?' he asked as he laid her down.

She summoned her most flirty smile and nodded. 'So much better.'

And then they were back to the game—but not quite. Because she lay in his arms and it was almost as before, his hands moving her hair from his face, then moving down to her arms and holding her, and yet she could hear the click of her thoughts in the silent air, and hoped he could not hear them too.

'That was bliss,' she said, trying to speak as she once had, to tone down the song in her heart.

She thought her world had changed when she'd met him. If she'd asked herself, she'd have named it as being then. But now, hearing the sound of his ragged breathing, seeing the look they were sharing, she felt as if they'd stumbled upon a new language. One only they knew or understood… And yet neither acknowledged it or denied it.

It hadn't been at the wedding.

Nor on boarding the plane.

Not even being alone in the desert.

For Violet they were all 'before'.

Now it was 'after'.

For the first time in her life she was completely in love.

And love made you brave.

'Can I stay?' She closed her eyes. 'I mean…'

Sahir felt her stiffen, as if braced for rejection, and from all she'd told him, from all he knew, he realised that Violet hadn't ever dared ask that question before.

'Just for a few more days?' she said.

He thought of her at the restaurant that first night, putting up her hand, not wanting a farewell speech. How she'd been prepared to leave that first morning.

She'd been forced to be independent. Had been let down over and over again. And he felt a great sense of responsibility as she now held out a piece of the heart that had been broken by so many.

'I can't leave you alone here,' he told her.

'I know.' She sat up. 'It was a silly idea. I was just…' She shrugged.

'Come to the palace.'

She swallowed.

'You would have to have your own wing, and it would be very different to here, but…' He refused to hide her—or, worse, send her away. 'I have to see King Abdul tomorrow. But we could meet for breakfast; you could have a day in the hammam…'

'Won't it cause problems?'

'You're a very nice problem to have.' He looked at her. 'Get dressed. I don't want the staff to find us in bed.'

As she climbed out, he couldn't help but smile at her oiled body and how she still hobbled a bit.

'Violet,' he said. 'You are my guest. Expect to be treated well.'

She gave a tentative nod, and as she went to her room to hurriedly dress he wanted to call her back. They needed to speak properly before they left for it would be impossible at the palace.

And it was impossible now, for he could hear their transport arriving.

Then it dawned on him.

He knew how they could speak.

His mother had taught him well…

Violet could hear terse conversation as she packed. She didn't need to be fluent in the language to know that Aadil was not best pleased.

Then all was silent, and she was terrified Sahir had changed his mind.

She picked up the poetry book, clutching it to her chest like a shield as she stepped out, but the tent was empty.

She went to replace the book in the trunk, but then knelt instead, picking up the Christmas menu she had found, turning it over, wondering if she should ask Sahir about it, or…

She felt too tumbled to think, so she just slipped it inside the book—then started when Aadil stepped into the living area.

'We depart shortly.'

'Fine.' Violet stood. 'I'm just going to say goodbye to Bedra.'

She went to walk off, but Aadil spoke again.

'It would be easier on him if you left.'

She said nothing.

'Just so you are aware.'

'I'm more than aware.' Violet turned around. 'You're the one who brought me here, Aadil.'

'At the King's command.'

Violet swallowed.

'Here in Janana we follow the rules.'

CHAPTER ELEVEN

VIOLET FOLLOWED THE RULES.

Desperate not to be like her parents, all her life she had followed the rules.

Yet something had changed, and now she refused to meekly surrender…to just nod and give up on love.

Not that she dared tell Sahir—after all, she knew how forbidden it was here, this love.

It was as the helicopter swept them across the desert that she accepted that.

The sun was a ball of orange fire as it lowered, and she looked over to Sahir, the first person she had ever truly given her heart to.

He sat opposite, staring out of the window, and she looked at his rough unshaven jaw and the mouth that could sink her to her knees. And then he turned and gave her a small smile— and, yes, she loved him.

Violet couldn't help but go misty-eyed at the sight of the palace from the sky. Last time she'd been too anxious to really take it all in, but now she truly didn't want to miss a thing.

Carved into the rocks—or from the rocks—it was incredible. Within the palace walls there was a beautiful central star, and from each point emerged a separate wing. From high up they looked like beams of light.

It was a fractured star, though, for as they hovered to de-

scend she could see the rubble and the ruins Sahir was fighting to have rebuilt.

A plane was on the runway when they landed—not the royal
plane that had brought her here, but the small dark one she had
seen on the runway in London.

Sahir's private jet was all prepared and waiting…

Gosh, they really did want her gone.

She briefly met Aadil's gaze and then flicked her eyes away,
feeling guilty at her own audacity in her refusal to leave.

She walked with Sahir, her stomach knotted as they passed
through a beautiful arch and the mechanical world of jets and
helicopters was left behind…

It was paradise—or it felt like it.

The sun was still low in the sky, and after the heat of the
desert there was the cool shade of trees. Little birds perched on
fountains, and huge butterflies hovered over flowers.

'It's beautiful,' she said.

'There are several gardens,' Sahir told her as they walked.
'This is the welcoming garden.'

'Really?' she asked with a slight edge, even as Aadil's eyes
shot daggers into her back.

'You *are* welcome,' Sahir said. 'You are my guest and do
not forget that.'

'Sahir. I'm sorry if this is—'

'Such a clear night,' he interrupted, glancing up at the sky.

She guessed they weren't allowed to discuss private matters.

'The view is magnificent from the Inanna wing,' he went
on. 'That means Venus.'

'What's your wing called?'

Pria let out a small cough beside them and she realised her
innocent question was not allowed either.

'I was just…' God, she always said the wrong thing. 'I can
never remember the planets,' she said as they walked.

She stopped her nervous chatter; nobody was really listening anyway.

Two guards opened some doors and bowed to Sahir.

They entered, stepping onto a stone floor. Embedded within it was a golden star, where a bearded man paced. She thought it must be the teller.

Her eyes were drawn upwards to the huge arches and stairs, and to a central tower that stretched so high she had to put her head fully back to see the top.

'The observatory is above us,' Sahir said, still being formal. 'Beyond the ceiling are the tower windows.'

'It's incredible...'

'Violet?'

She pulled her chin down at the sound of her name and smiled at Pria.

'Bibi will take you to the Venus wing.'

She looked at Sahir, uncertain when she would see him again.

'Tomorrow we shall take breakfast in the East Garden before I leave, and then you can visit the hammam,' Sahir told her.

'Sounds wonderful.' She smiled. 'How do I get to the East Garden?'

It was Pria who responded. 'I shall come and collect you.' She turned to Sahir. 'The King is waiting to brief you on the agenda for tomorrow with King Abdul.'

'Of course.'

He nodded, and then there was a sudden stir—a slight flutter of panic from everyone except Sahir.

It was the arrival of the King.

'Sahir...' His father paused abruptly as he locked eyes with their unexpected guest.

Thankfully Violet copied Pria and bowed, grateful for her hurried advice.

'Respond only if he speaks...just light chit-chat.'

'Yes...' Violet breathed, as she came up to stand. At least she was good at that.

'Sahir, we have a meeting.' The King's eyes fell on Violet. 'Miss Lewis.'

'Your Majesty…'

'King Babek,' he invited. 'I trust you enjoyed your time in the desert?'

'Very much,' Violet said, and heard Aadil's low voice in her ear telling her to thank him.

Sahir watched as they all waited for Violet's suitable response. Never had he hated the stilted atmosphere of the palace more. He was tempted to open one of the arched windows and let her escape.

'The desert was wonderful,' Violet said. 'The flight there was a little hair-raising, but apart from that…'

Sahir suppressed a smile, certain that his father would simply stalk off. Yet he remained.

'You're from London?'

'I am.'

Sahir saw Violet's lips tremble as she smiled, but King Babek had already moved his attention to Sahir.

'How was Carter's wedding?'

'Excellent,' Sahir said, knowing damn well his father was reminding them both that it had been there that they'd met, and less than a week ago.

'I have fond memories of London,' King Babek said, and Sahir almost exhaled in relief. This was the polite, quiet conclusion to his brief greeting.

'Yes,' Violet said, clearly missing the signal that the King was about to leave. 'I saw a gorgeous photo of you there with the Queen.'

Nobody had been moving, but even so Violet felt everyone still. She knew she had spoken out of turn as she saw the King's eyes flare, and then she realised her mistake.

'The late Queen,' she hurriedly corrected, and then with

slight horror realised her further mistake. 'I mean, *my* late queen. Queen Elizabeth…'

'Of course.' The King actually gave a small laugh, but then made it clear he was done. 'Goodnight, Miss Lewis.'

Damn! She screwed up her face as he walked off.

'Violet?' Sahir's calm voice allowed her to open her eyes. 'Well done.'

'I shouldn't have…'

'I have to go.' They looked right into each other's eyes, because here that was all they could do. 'I'll see you in the morning.'

'Yes.'

'You can stop smiling now,' he said gently, and Violet nodded, remembering the night they had met when he'd taken her into the garden.

She was brave, Sahir thought as she walked off into the unknown.

'The King is ready,' Aadil informed him.

'Thank you.'

He knew a measured approach was needed with his father, and that emotion had no place inside these stone walls.

It had arrived, though, Sahir knew.

He'd just have to hide it for now—get through this meeting, remain icily calm.

'Your Highness…'

Hakaam stepped out of the star and Sahir stood politely as the teller, as always, briefed him on the skies before his meeting with the King.

'Neptune is in conjunction with Mercury. There may be deception…'

'I see.'

'Irrational thinking. Emotions flaring.'

'Thank you.' Sahir gave him a polite smile.

There would be no emotions flaring. He'd face his father with calm, and go through tomorrow's schedule.

Violet was referred to only once.

'Your guest is very talkative,' his father said.

'And very forgiving,' Sahir said. 'I could think of words other than "hair-raising" to describe her journey to the desert.'

'I did what I could to give you a short holiday.'

Sahir looked up and met the challenge of his father's eyes, which were as cold as black ice, in a face he'd barely seen smile.

This could have been him in twenty years' time, Sahir knew. It might have been him had Violet not come into his life, warm and effusive, volatile…

Perhaps Hakaam was correct.

His thoughts were somewhat irrational, he knew, for he was glimpsing a future—and not the one he was destined for.

'It's time to get back to business, Sahir.'

'I understand.'

He saw Aadil's stance relax a little, and his father's nod—only Sahir had not yet finished talking.

'Of course it would have been remiss to send a junior royal to meet with King Abdul. However, I *shall* resume my leave on my return.' He turned the page on his schedule. 'Let's move things along.'

Sahir wanted this meeting closed.

There was somewhere else he needed to be.

Oh, why did she always say the wrong thing?

Pria was very prim as she opened the door to the Venus wing. 'This way, Violet.'

It was bewildering to walk through a palace where love was forbidden. To walk into a suite and be braced for something cold and formal, yet find it was so beautiful her breath caught. The stone walls were a soft blue hue, and gorgeous lights hung like stars.

'A light supper?' Pria said.

A small table was dressed with silver and candlelit. It was inviting and opulent and Violet stood there, resisting the urge to say *wow*. To gape.

'Wow!' She couldn't help it. 'It's…' She looked at the sapphire and silver. 'So beautiful…'

'It is the alignments tonight.' Pria smiled. 'Prince Sahir thought you might want something to eat.'

'Thank you.'

'There are robes and perfumes for you to use, and I have arranged the hammam for you tomorrow, but first I shall take you to breakfast with the Prince. I have to go to the meeting now.' She gave Violet a lovely smile. 'You were fine.'

'I was dreadful.'

'Oh, no.' Pria shook her head. 'You should have heard Sahir when he found out what had happened. And I must say I told both Sahir and the King that I was not happy…'

'You were very kind to me that day,' Violet said, and was glad of the chance to thank her.

Pria left then, and Violet slipped off her shoes, thinking of what Sahir had said.

She could stop smiling now.

The supper was welcome, but best of all was the silver tray of chocolates which she put by her bed. She showered and came out wrapped in a towel, wondering if she should have brought the nightdress from the desert.

She pulled open a few doors, but saw nothing to wear, then finally found a cupboard full of gowns—but clearly they were meant for daytime.

She ran her hand down one. It was sapphire-coloured, like the wax catcher on the candelabra, and it was far too stunning to sleep in. But she could hardly sleep in the nude.

A candle might get knocked over, Violet thought, imagining a fire in the night and another awkward encounter with the King.

She pulled it over her naked body.

Oh, it felt like velvet against her skin…

She stared into a long free-standing mirror and saw herself for the first time since the desert… There had only been hand mirrors there.

Her hair was lighter, just from that ride in the sun, but that wasn't the only change…

She looked at her breasts. She wore no bra, and the sapphire gown clung. Her nipples grew erect just at the memory of that afternoon.

No, she could never be Queen—and not just because of her lack of status.

More because of her love for Sahir and how she ached to see him.

She wondered how they'd be at breakfast…sitting apart, unable to touch.

The poetry book was by the bed, and rather than get under the sheets she lay on top, bringing a candle to the bedside.

'You'll ruin your eyes, Violet,' she warned herself, biting into a bitter chocolate.

She cringed all over again when she thought of what she'd said to the King.

Oh, it wasn't so much the hair-raising bit where she'd messed up, it was mentioning his late wife…

She thought of his flare of anger as she'd spoken out of turn. No, not anger…

Violet shook her head, refusing to think about it and turned to a very dog-eared page in the book.

Pablo Neruda
Every Day You Play…

Boring, she decided. She didn't want to read about playing. But there were a lot of notes in the margin, so she gave it a go.

Oh, my…!

It was very sensual.

It was not a poem to read when you'd been thoroughly made love to and now had to spend the night alone.

Queen Anousheh's notes and underscores explained it better than any teacher, and the poem made the cold night air feel like a midday furnace.

Violet read of suffering and savage, solitary souls, and thought of Sahir—and then she thought that absolutely she was ordering this book when she got home…

Then she lay back, wondering if she'd let him down, but then she recalled his dark eyes as he told her she could relax, as he had that first night. She could stop smiling now.

'It's just us.'

It wasn't, though. They were an entire palace apart. She didn't even know which wing he was in…

It didn't matter, Violet suddenly realised, opening her eyes and slowly sitting up.

He'd been telling her about the observatory, the clear night, the view.

Sahir hadn't been being formal.

He'd been telling her where they could meet.

Hadn't he?

Opening her bedroom door, she peered down the long corridor. There was a maid sitting at the end.

'Goodnight,' Violet said, and slunk back inside.

Then she looked up at the ceiling, but there was no clue there. Then her gaze came down, and she looked at the many doors, one with a yellow gold and silver circle embedded in it…

Venus.

Inanna.

There seemed to be just a brick wall behind it, but then she saw that there was the same gold and silver circle embedded on the other side.

Violet picked up the candle and peered into the void. She saw that to one side there was a set of steep stairs.

It was creepy, and the candelabra was so heavy. And then it puffed out, so she left it on the first turn.

What if she was wrong?

She persisted on the slim chance that she was right.

She climbed up, ever up, and then she came to a door. Pushing it open, she came to a platform with four small arched windows and the whole of Janana stretched out below…

'Hey!'

He startled her. She was breathless from the climb.

'You…' she gasped, and then his arms were around her waist, as he held her from behind. 'I'm sorry if I said the wrong thing back there.'

'Stop,' he told her, lifting her hair, his hands on her breasts, naked beneath the sapphire gown. 'I've been thinking of you.'

His mouth was hot on her neck, his hands rough, pinching her nipples. And then his hot palms smoothed over her breasts, making her ache for the fabric to dissolve, so much… He was slipping a hand in the neckline. Only it was too high…

His growl was impatient as he dropped contact, and then took her wrist to guide her back to the stairwell.

'What if we get caught?' she asked.

'We won't if we're quiet.'

'But…'

His jaw gritted, and he looked at her, and she saw the glint in the eyes of a man who did not want to sneak like a thief in his home, even if it was a palace.

She watched him walk to the door she'd just come through, and he lifted the latch on the heavy bolt. She heard the scrape of it closing.

'It's just us,' he said.

She smiled.

The moon was behind her and she could see her own shadow on the stone wall. She stood, aroused, flushed and breathless, as he approached.

He gathered her into him, his body a wedge of muscle. His

tongue prised open her mouth, and she kissed him back with all her might.

'I thought…'

She was panting, on the edge of crying at the final bliss of this day, at how she'd thought she'd be on her way home.

'We can't last,' she said, as his hands clasped her bottom. 'I know that.'

She was frantic. His hands had pulled up the velvet material and she could feel the cold night air on her bottom as she searched for the opening in his robe.

'Sahir…'

She did not know it could be this urgent—that she would choose a cold stone stairwell to be devoured in, rather than be made love to under a starry sky.

Their mouths were one…his hands were still on her bottom, pressing in and then stroking.

'Take me…' she said, and he lifted her. 'Ow,' she said, for the muscles of her inner thighs were too taut to stretch.

And yet they did so, because she ordered them to, wrapping her legs around him, sobbing as he smoothly entered her. Her back was to the wall and he was wild, tearing the front of the sapphire robe. His mouth was hot on her breast, and then he moved it back to her lips. That was foreplay, and all she required.

'I want to…' She held on to him. She wanted to stay. She did not want to be sent home. She was sobbing as he took her.

'Sahir…'

She was ready to beg him to keep her. His body was hard and his breathing ragged. The tension of him untamed was bringing her to the edge of honesty.

'Please let me stay. I'll be your lover…your concubine. I'll be—'

'Shh…'

His hand came over her mouth and she licked his palm. He thrust into her hard, and then he stilled, and it was Sahir who let out a low shout that must startle the skies because it was primal.

Violet was climaxing so deeply that it almost hurt. Even her thighs contracted as he spilled inside her. It was everything she needed, all she desired, and she kissed his mouth.

She felt his firm hands lowering her down and she leant against him, his arms and body the only things that kept her standing.

Somehow she had to forget what she'd discovered today.

How much she loved Sahir.

CHAPTER TWELVE

THEY WENT UP to the observatory.

Her legs were shaky from the sex, and from the endless excitement he brought to her soul.

'You should first see the stars lying down,' Sahir told her as they reached the top. 'Close your eyes.'

She stood, eyes closed, and felt it was oddly silent. The echoes from the stairwell were gone, and the air was very cool. She could feel it on her exposed breasts. He took her hand and she walked on cold stone.

'When did you work it out?' he asked.

'I was reading on the bed…' She paused, frowning, as beneath her feet she suddenly felt a soft rug.

'Keep your eyes closed and lower yourself.'

She wanted to feel behind her, but she held his hands and lowered herself down—not to a cold, hard floor, but onto a soft cushion.

'How…?'

'No questions,' Sahir said. 'Lie back.'

It was disorientating. Her body was braced to be lying on stone, but instead she felt enveloped in silk.

Violet lay waiting as he joined her and took her in his arms. 'Can I look now?'

'When you are ready.'

She could never have been ready.

Violet opened her eyes, and nothing could have prepared her for the feast in the sky. There were more stars than she could even begin to count. Everywhere her eyes fell there were more, yet more, and everything she'd thought she knew or believed, or didn't know and did not believe, vanished—because she was staring at something so impossible, so divine, it was impossible not to lie there in awe. The sight was impossible to fathom... silvers, pinks, blues, gold. Endless beauty.

'I'll never forget this,' Violet said, gazing into the magnificence. 'How do you even begin to learn about them?'

'Hakaam is the last of his school. He was one of seven. They learned from ancient almanacs, or calendars, first written in clay. Even as he passes on his knowledge, they still discover more.'

He showed her the stars, some planets...

'Spica...' He guided her to the tiny light. 'That is actually two stars—maybe more—so close together, orbiting each other.'

'How close?'

'Eleven million miles apart.'

Unfathomable.

Like them.

'I know we can't last,' she said again, staring up to the sky. 'I know that, but I wouldn't change things.'

'You're a pessimist.'

'Yes.'

'What happened to sunny, happy Violet?'

'I don't have to be her when I'm with you.'

'You don't.'

'I'm scared you'll marry and bring your wife to visit Carter and Grace...'

'Violet.' He halted her. 'Can I ask you to trust me enough to know that I shall sort this out?'

'I don't see how.'

'Nor do I yet,' Sahir admitted. 'You're a very new puzzle.'

She turned to look at him, and he truly was as stunning as the sky. 'I'm scared I'll only be your lover.'

'Do you really think I'd want that?'

'Yes.' Violet nodded. 'If that's the only way.'

She sat up and tucked up her knees, looked at all the lovely cushions and rugs. There were even jugs and glasses and little sweet treats.

'Did the maids do this?'

'No, my mother taught me. I didn't realise it at the time, but she was teaching me all the secret places…'

'To take a lover?'

'She was romantic. I guess she wanted me to be too.'

'Well, she taught you well.'

'I'm furious with my father, Violet,' he admitted. 'We have never got on, but we have always worked together well. I don't see how we can now.'

'You have to.'

'I don't know… He should know better than to mess with my private life.'

'It's not just him, Sahir, it's the council, the elders… Of course they want you married to someone suitable to have heirs.'

'I told them maybe when I am forty.'

She inhaled sharply, understanding now what he'd been saying that first night, and she hated it that she cried. Because five years from now…

'Come here.' He pulled her down into his arms as she cried, and it felt nice. 'I'm going to fight for us,' he told her.

She gave a mirthless, tear-choked laugh and tried to pull away. 'I don't believe you, Sahir. Nobody's ever fought to keep me.'

It was, Sahir knew, going to take more than a few nights to wipe out a lifetime of hurt for her. And even though he didn't tell her, Sahir could not see how.

They slept, bathed by the stars, and in his arms she was perfection.

Sunrise woke him.

Sahir looked at Violet's soft, round cheeks. They were usually pink, sometimes blushing, occasionally pale with anger, even fear, like when she'd first bravely faced him here. This morning, though...

He could not quite say. Perhaps they were the palest pink, and yet she was glowing. The desert sun had added little freckles to her nose, and as he put up a hand and touched her cheek it felt like a soft petal...

'Morning...' she said.

'We have to go,' Sahir said. 'Pria will be arriving to escort you to breakfast soon.'

'That's right.'

They had to hide all the cushions in some cupboards and he locked them away.

'Did your mother teach you that too?'

'She did.' He rolled his eyes. 'She was a bit...wild.'

'She was wonderful,' Violet said. 'Well, her taste in poetry was impeccable. There was one I read last night...' Violet stopped.

'Please don't tell me any more about my mother's private life.'

'I won't.'

Only that hadn't been the reason she'd stopped talking. Her head was spinning as she thought about the words in that poem as Sahir led her down the stairs. So much so that she went to the wrong entrance and was about to press the handle.

'Violet!' He halted her, pointed to the gold sun etched into the door. 'That would take you to my father's wing.'

'Whoops!'

'Hurry! Have a quick wash and put on a fresh robe. Pria is always early.'

She was right about the meaning of that poem, Violet was certain. And even though she had to get ready for Pria, she was barely inside her room before she opened the poetry book and found the earmarked page.

This poem Anousheh had loved so, Violet had been so sure it was about the King…

Yet she frowned and read the lines again.

Or was it *from* the King?

'Sahir…' She dipped a piece of fruit in some honey as they shared a breakfast in the garden. 'Do you think your parents ever…?'

He looked over.

'Used the secret staircases?'

'Violet!' He laughed at the very notion.

'Only…' She stopped as more tea was poured and knew this really wasn't the place to have this conversation.

'What?'

'Nothing.' She smiled. 'When is your flight?'

'When I board,' he said, and then conceded. 'Now.' He stood as Pria approached. 'You'll be okay?'

'Of course.'

'Go to the hammam,' he suggested. 'If you still ache.'

'Oh, I do.'

He did not kiss her goodbye, but she didn't need it to feel the warmth in his parting, and she knew he would come to her tonight, in the observatory.

Violet took her time to finish her breakfast, then went to stand at a huge arch as Sahir and his entourage walked through the Welcome Gardens, lingering to watch the royal jet soar into the sky.

Nervous about the future, she still dared to feel happy. She even wore a smile on her face as she walked through the central star and glanced up, thinking of last night and more certain with each step that she was right about Queen Anousheh.

Pushing the door open to her wing, she walked down the long corridor, then turned into her suite.

'Bibi?'

She frowned, because the maid was crying. She met the unwelcome glare of Aadil.

'What's going on…?'

'I was just moving your glass,' Bibi sobbed.

Violet felt her heart plummet as she glanced down at the floor and saw the scattered stones—diamonds, emeralds and rubies—and the little square of silk Sahir had given to her the first day they'd met.

It was her worst nightmare…

'What's going on?'

She heard both Layla's voice and her footsteps.

'Oh…' Her face fell when she saw the jewels.

'They are Queen Anousheh's,' Aadil said. 'I believe they have been missing for some time.' As Layla went to scoop them up, he halted her. 'Don't touch them. We've called for the palace jeweller.'

Violet, when she should be protesting her innocence, was shivering.

'I found them in the trunk.' She felt as if she might vomit. 'I left them there.'

She wasn't crying or pleading, which astounded her, and she just let Layla take her by the shoulders and sit her down.

'It's a simple mistake.' Layla glared at Aadil. 'Please leave us.'

'Not till the palace jeweller is here.'

It was dreadful—the awful silence as the jeweller arrived and with white gloves collected the stones, each and every one. It took ages.

Aadil took the square of silk.

Oh, why didn't she say something? State her case?

Because it was hopeless.

She didn't want to see the doubt in Sahir's eyes, or the disappointment—or, on the impossible chance that he believed her, watch him having to defend her. To people who wanted her gone.

'It's a misunderstanding,' Layla said, when all had left.

'Why aren't you with Sahir?' asked Violet.

'I'm on my day off.' Layla smiled and took her cold hands. 'It's okay, you're shocked. I am going to contact Pria. She can tell Sahir—'

'No.' Violet shook her head. 'Please don't.'

'He has to know.'

'Not yet.' She shook her head again. 'Not until I've gone.'

'Violet? There's no need for that.'

'I'm not running away. If the police need to see me…'

'No police.'

'I just want to go home,' she said. 'As soon as possible. Can that be arranged, or should I do it myself?'

'It can be arranged.' Layla nodded sadly. 'Of course.'

'Thank you.'

She sat there for ages. Layla kept bringing tea, and even offered her some brandy.

'I don't like brandy.' Violet stood. 'I might go for a walk. Get some air before the flight.'

'The pilot will be here in an hour, but you can still change your mind.'

'I won't.'

No, she'd spent a lifetime under a cloud of suspicion, and she was not living like that again. Furthermore, even as they'd made love last night, she'd known it was too wonderful to last.

She picked up the book, wanting to bury her face in something rather than actually read, just to see the next hour out.

She wandered blindly around the fragrant gardens, barely noticing the gorgeous blooms, wishing she'd known this morning that it would be their final goodbye.

Then she looked ahead and saw a man sitting beneath the shade of a tree and her heart stopped. For a tiny second she'd thought it was Sahir, but it was the King, sitting alone…

'Your Majesty.'

'This is my private garden,' he snarled.

'I got lost…' She took a breath. 'I'm leaving shortly. I wanted to say thank you.'

He huffed and waved her away. Only she found he didn't scare her out here. Given where she'd visited her father, a pretty garden with one angry man really didn't daunt her.

'Leave me in peace,' he snapped.

'Of course,' Violet said, and turned to walk away.

But then she looked at him, so upright and so rigid, so hostile.

So lonely?

'I found something.'

'I heard.'

He gave a mirthless laugh, and Violet knew he was referring to the jewels.

'It's a menu. I thought it might have been misplaced. I didn't know if I should ask Sahir, or just ignore it, or…'

He looked over at her as she opened the poetry book and took out the folded card she'd slipped inside.

His hand was trembling a little as she handed the cream sheet of paper to him, and she swore that in those dark eyes there was the shimmer of tears. And then a smile had the years falling from his features, and the agony, and the grief…

'Where did you find this?'

'In the same trunk as those jewels—which were then planted in my room to put Sahir off me.' The King glanced sideways. 'Anyway, I found it in there. It's a Christmas menu from the Savoy. There are little ticks…the Queen's writing.' Violet watched as he traced the handwriting. 'She kept a lot of things.'

'I didn't know.'

And suddenly Violet was brave—perhaps because she was leaving. 'That's the Christmas before Sahir was born.'

The King didn't move, didn't blink, but she felt the silence in the quiet garden and knew he did not need to read the date on the lavish card. He recalled it exactly.

'Have you told Sahir?'

'Of course not.'

'Not yet?' he said accusingly. 'If you are here to blackmail me, don't bother. The elders would crush you—and anyway, who would care now?'

'I don't blackmail people,' Violet told him, and knew that his threats were not really aimed at her, but born of fear. For if she had guessed correctly then this must be such a secret. 'And I certainly haven't told Sahir.'

'You will,' he accused.

'No.' Violet shook her head. 'It's not my secret to share.' She stood still, thinking of the huge secret she had stumbled upon. 'He ought to be told, though.'

'Never.'

'I thought as much. Would you like to…?'

'What?'

'Well, if you haven't been able to talk about it with any-one…' She knew that must hurt. 'I would never say anything,' Violet blurted out, and was rewarded with a disbelieving laugh.

She had been like that once—as a little girl she had smiled and laughed, but it had been an act. Inside she'd been pinched, refusing to trust a soul. Eventually, while she'd still guarded a lot of her heart, she had learnt to trust certain people—like Grace, Mrs Andrews before she'd got ill, an especially kind social worker, and lately Sahir.

Especially Sahir.

She had trusted her body to him…her heart. But, more, he had taught her to trust another person.

Herself.

That was Sahir's gift to her, Violet realised. Trust in her own judgement. And that made her brave enough to persist—not with 'the King', but with this man who sat alone on the bench.

'It must be hard not to talk about the times you two shared,' she suggested gently. 'I will have to go home and lie to my best friend…pretend I didn't spend my time here having the most wonderful time.'

'If she's your best friend, why can't you tell her?'

'Because I don't want to place her in the position of not telling her husband. And I don't want things to be awkward in the future.' Violet took a breath. 'I am guessing Carter and Sahir will remain friends, and that means we'll see each other on occasion.' She could feel tears trickling down the back of her throat, but she swallowed them down. 'Sahir and I agreed on the night we met to keep things just between us.'

The King remained silent, and Violet didn't blame him for not trusting her.

'Your Majesty…' She nodded her head and was just about to walk off when the King suddenly spoke.

'We met at a debating competition in London. Our universities were in the final.' He gave a hollow laugh. 'My father was surprised when I put my hand up to do that.'

Violet smiled.

'We managed one day alone. She wanted to try a British Christmas dinner.' He laughed. 'We thought mince pies would at least have meat in them, but instead they were filled with fruit.'

'I can't stand them,' Violet told him.

She imagined expecting a mince pie to be full of meat, instead of sweet fruit, and it made her laugh.

The King reluctantly laughed too. 'There was Christmas pudding…'

'Yuk.'

He smiled.

'Did you enjoy the meal?'

'I can't say the food was quite as I expected. But it was still the best meal of my life,' he said fondly. 'There were consequences, though…'

She guessed that meant Sahir! 'A long lunch, then!'

He smiled at her cheeky response.

'A very long lunch,' he agreed.

He did not say they'd married because of Sahir, but it was very clear…

'There was a lot of urgent discussion, the council met and with help from a couple of very select people my bride was "chosen". Believe me, with all the unrest between our countries she would not normally have been considered. Except then…' His voice grew husky. 'She was the most wonderful queen. She brought passion and vigorous debate into every room, but peace into the desert and the gardens.'

'Yet you hid your love? Even from your children?'

'We had to. The King's promise to the country is for a steady ruler, free from emotional ties to any other.' He halted. 'Very few people knew the truth, and they helped keep our secret at great personal risk.'

'Can I ask something?' Violet said, because truly she didn't understand. 'You loved your wife very much?'

'Yes.'

'Yet you don't want the same love for your own children?'

'Anousheh did. She had many projects, and changing the laws regarding marriage was one of her priorities. She knew it would be an uphill fight—we both knew.' He grew serious then. 'I always thought it was just nonsense, having to hide like a thief to be with my wife, having to treat her like a colleague. Yet, after I lost my queen I was…'

He said some words in Arabic.

'It means distracted…wandering,' he told Violet. He looked at her. 'There is a reason why love is not always wise. I was lost for at least two years. At the time there was a lot of instability with some neighbouring countries. Had it not been for the guidance of Aadil and his father I might have made some less than wise choices.'

He shook his head.

'I never want that kind of danger for my people.' He glanced over at her. 'To lead a troubled country when grieving is an agony… I wouldn't wish that on an enemy, let alone my son. You can support him quietly, be there, but…'

'Not fully?'

'Correct.' He nodded. 'I'm offering you a compromise.'

'I'm tired of compromising.'

Violet stared at her hands, placed together in her lap, recalling Sahir's fingers closed around her own. She gripped her own fingers tighter, offering her own support to herself.

'Your son has taught me that I deserve better than to be second best.'

'Think about it.'

'I want a family of my own,' Violet said. 'It's all I've ever wanted. And, while Queen Anousheh sounds incredible, I'm no good at debate, nor playing on the other side.'

'Will you tell Sahir?'

'No. I gave you my word.'

Violet wanted to tell him that that he, too, had been entitled to love, but his secret was too big and so she shook her head. She thought of Sahir…how he hated the memory of that final conversation he'd had with his mother…how he loathed Aadil, when in truth, he was on their side.

'I do wish you'd tell him,' she said.

'No.'

'Please?'

'I said no.' The King was clearly regretting that this conversation had even taken place. 'What time is your flight?'

'Soon.'

Violet stood there, sad and defeated, because she did not know how to fight, how to be mean, how to persuade another person just to get what she wanted. But she would stand up for Sahir.

'He told his mother off,' she told the King. 'That was the

last conversation he had with her. He was trying to protect her from being caught…' But, no, she could never play mean. 'You have my word, Your Majesty.'

CHAPTER THIRTEEN

SAHIR DID NOT walk from the royal jet.

He strode.

Not to his father's office, but to the Venus wing. Hakaam didn't halt him with his predictions or warnings. He just stood by the star, wringing his hands.

It was grief. Sahir knew that as he stepped into the bedroom suite...

There were the gowns she had worn still hanging, and he picked up the book by her bed, hurt for her because she hadn't taken it.

Opening it, he saw his mother's name—and closed it abruptly.

'You can be so staid at times.' He could almost hear her voice. *'Just like your father.'*

No.

He was not staid. Had not been staid from the second Violet had arrived in his life. He preferred himself now...missed her more than he knew how to miss another person.

And she was the priority.

It could be no other way.

The people would understand—or not.

Simply, it was right.

So he stood and walked away at pace.

Hakaam was still pacing around the star, and when he saw the direction Sahir was taking he pounced. 'Your Highness...'

'Not now,' Sahir barked. 'I have to speak with the King.'

'The planets in fire are misaligned. There is no harmony,' Hakaam urged. 'Please show restraint...'

'Too late.'

He parted the guards and walked past Aadil, and it was the King who hurriedly asked for the room to be cleared.

'You have no idea what you've done.' The doors had barely closed before he told his father the consequences of his actions. 'The jet is being refuelled. I leave for London as soon as the pilots are here.'

'You cannot leave now,' the King said. 'It's not possible.'

'It's what is happening. I am leaving tonight. I shall discuss my schedule later, but for now I shall be in London, sorting out the mess you have made. I might marry there—if she can forgive what has occurred.'

'Any marriage would be void here.'

'Then I shall be a bitter, lonely ruler like you—save for the times when I am overseas.'

'What about heirs?'

'That is a matter for you and the council.'

'They would never agree. They would demand your banishment.'

'I shall not go voluntarily—you would have to rescind my titles. Know this, though: you will get to explain why I am overseas. How dare Aadil plant those jewels?'

'She was caught red-handed,' the King sneered.

Sahir's curse told his father what he thought of that.

'Look...' the King said, and he opened a file, handed Sahir a sheaf of papers clipped to a photo of Violet on the balcony. 'Take a look...'

'I don't need to.'

'Of course you do!'

Sahir skimmed through the papers, his throat tightening as he realised how Violet had toned down the horrors of her childhood for him. He now learned that she had been taken from her parents at birth, rehomed over and over, then sent out alone into the world at sixteen.

'Hardly impressive reading,' his father said.

'On the contrary,' Sahir said. 'I find it very impressive that, despite all that, Violet is warm and strong.'

'She didn't even finish school.'

Sahir put down the file. 'I believe you yourself said never to mistake education for intelligence.'

'Her father has been repeatedly jailed. It's reprehensible!'

'Yes, both Violet and I have fathers whose behaviour has been reprehensible.' Sahir came right up to his face. 'It's brought us closer.'

'You are infatuated,' the King said. 'You are in *love*.'

Sahir drew in a breath.

Hakaam might well be right, he thought. Restraint was required. Because to admit to love would be the death knell for both of them. It would mean that Violet could never be his wife.

'I'm going to London.'

'Sahir, please take another look at the photo.'

Angrily he swiped up the file and looked at the image—and then he understood why Hakaam had been pacing, for perhaps this really was a most perilous moment.

'Look at you, Sahir,' said the King.

His eyes moved to his own image. He was in the background, standing by the French windows, watching Violet. Her arms were raised...she was soaking in the morning. He barely recognised his own features, the look in his eyes, the soft smile he wore...

His father had known before he had.

'Love is a poor decision-maker,' his father said. 'An Achilles heel—a weakness that can be manipulated. Our people have suffered enough for that. Their king—'

'I'm aware of what happened, and why the laws are in place. How my mother suffered for them.'

'What did she say to you?' He watched his father's features darken. 'Your lover is both a thief and a liar.'

'She's neither,' Sahir said. 'I haven't spoken to Violet. I don't need to, to know.'

'Your mother did not suffer.'

'Oh, no? I'll tell you this. If you had—' He pulled back from the edge. From talking about the bruises his father had dismissed. His own guilt clashed within him as he fought not to lay blame. 'Don't lecture me about love.'

Sahir turned away.

'You can't leave now.'

'Watch me.'

Sahir walked to the huge doors, expecting his father to call him back—which he did. But he had never anticipated the words he would choose.

'I am to undergo surgery.'

The King let that sink in for just a moment, watching his eldest son, the most composed of men, recover from only the briefest falter and then turn around.

'It is delicate surgery…neurological…'

'You didn't think to tell me?'

'I had an…episode a couple of weeks ago.'

'And?'

'Aadil thought it should be checked out.'

'No.' Sahir shook his head. 'Aadil would never have left you and come to London if you were ill…'

'It didn't seem that serious then. I was just…'

'More worried than you let on to Aadil?' Sahir said. 'So it was time to push ahead on my marriage…' He frowned. 'What happened on Saturday?'

'I don't know what you are referring to.'

'Don't lie now.'

'A small seizure. Hakaam overreacted and hit the panic alarm.'

'I should have been informed.'

'I myself have only just found out the extent of the…growth.'

'Growth?' He stood, stunned, watching his father discuss a brain tumour and his possible demise in such a matter-of-fact fashion.

'I want to go into surgery knowing the future is taken care of. I want you married to a suitable bride—not giddy with love. I have fought hard to give you a peaceful land to rule over.'

'Are you dying?'

'We'll know more after the surgery. Or you'll know more and I'll be gone…'

'You cold bastard.' Sahir stood. 'How can you tell me like this?' Then he looked at this man who had once so coldly sanctioned his aide to tell a teenager his mother had died. 'Does it never enter your head that I might care?'

'Sahir, this is not a time to be weak. I am explaining why you cannot leave.'

'Do you know why I'm going to ask Violet to marry me?' Sahir's voice was like a knife. 'Because I want everything my mother never had. I want my children to laugh with their father. Not to stand and be told he is dying as if he is simply getting a new robe.'

'I am not scared of death.'

'Good for you.'

'Sahir!' His father called him back. 'Clearly you cannot leave now.'

'You don't get to play the emotions card when you have none,' Sahir said. 'The only way I stay is if I can marry the woman I love.'

'The elders would never accept her.'

'Then see that they do. If Violet is to return, I won't keep her hidden. One day, she *will* be Queen…'

'Sahir—'

He wasn't listening. He was walking out. But then he heard the crack in his father's voice.

'Do not walk out…please…'

Sahir heard that ever-steady voice tremble, and on a day he had not thought could get any worse it simply did.

'How can I fear dying when I will be with my beloved Anousheh once again?'

'Father…?'

And then he watched as his father beat himself with the same stick Sahir had beaten himself with for decades.

'She had bruises… I should have insisted she get checked out.'

'No,' Sahir said, a little awkwardly putting an arm around his father.

'I did love her—and she loved me.'

'What are you saying?'

'Ask Violet…' his father sobbed. 'She knows your mother was loved.'

'Are you having another episode?' Sahir asked, in all seriousness. 'How on earth can she know?'

'She's so easy to talk to…'

Oh, she was.

And never had Sahir missed her more.

CHAPTER FOURTEEN

YOU'VE BEEN THROUGH WORSE.

Violet repeated this to herself over and over.

The world wasn't scary without Sahir.

It wasn't impossible either.

She just didn't like it as much.

She refused to limp through the week. She smiled and chatted with the regulars at the library, and told everyone about Grace's incredible wedding—oh, and although she didn't share the location, or the company she'd kept, she told them about her horse-riding lessons and made her colleagues laugh,

She'd changed her mobile number at Heathrow and regretted it already, but it was done.

She checked online all the time. To see if there was any gossip from Janana…anything…

Nothing.

It was her final day of work and she pulled on a tight skirt, and a dark blouse, and somehow she felt strong.

But also sad.

Especially when she saw some drooping tulips in the window of the local florist.

They look like me…

There was a place inside her that could never quite be healed. This loss hurt more than anything else ever had, and she hoped she would never hurt more, but she was above all tough.

And she was loved.

Mrs Hunt was dabbing her eyes. She knew the decision to let Violet go had been impossible.

'Don't cry.' She hugged her wonderful boss. 'I'm going to be fine.'

Her heart was pummelled but her spirit was strong. She'd ended the lease on her flat, applied for new and exciting jobs, and made Persian Love Cake for her own party.

She even gave a little speech.

'I don't want to leave, but the truth is if I hadn't been pushed I'd never have gone,' Violet said. 'Which means I'd have ended up watching you all leave…'

It wasn't a very good speech, but today it was the best she could do.

'I love you all—and thank you.'

And that was that.

She dragged the ladder to the poetry section, determined to find something at least similar to the book Anousheh had had.

She couldn't find anything like it, though, and close to tears, halfway up the ladder, she felt herself sway slightly.

'Careful.'

She felt hands on her hips, and any other touch would have made her jump. But never his. Always his touch felt steadying, as if it were a part of her…as if it was helping her right herself.

'Slowly,' Sahir said, guiding her down the steps and turning her to face him. 'You are very pale.'

'I've been on a diet.'

'Diet?' He frowned. 'Why?'

'A health kick.'

'So healthy you faint up ladders?' he scolded.

He was all shaved and suited, and she had to force herself to look at him. 'I didn't take those jewels.'

'I know that.'

She blinked.

'Had you not dumped your phone, you'd know that.'

'I honestly didn't—'

'Violet, stop. I'm not here about that. I would like to invite you to dinner.'

'No, thank you.'

'You are refusing?'

'Yes,' Violet said. 'We've had a big lunch for my leaving…' But she refused to lie. 'I'm saying no because I don't want to spend the rest of my life wondering if you are in London, or if you might drop in… Anyway, it won't matter soon. I'm moving.'

'I shall always seek you out.'

'Kidnap *and* stalking…' Her eyes narrowed. 'Are you married yet?'

'No.'

'Engaged?'

'We don't have engagements.'

'Oh, that's right—no romance. So, is there a wedding planned?'

'Not yet.'

And she was weakening…wanting to know. 'Has your bride been chosen?'

'I am not discussing such issues here,' Sahir said. 'Let's have dinner later. There is a car outside that will take you home to prepare.'

'Hardly spontaneous…'

'I want to dine with the woman I first met.' He looked down at her drab skirt and blouse, and then to her pale cheeks and lips. 'Not her shadow.'

'Her shadow,' Violet said, 'is the sexy one.'

He smiled, and it was such a treat to see it, such a contrast to the severe man she'd met.

'Very well, I'll come to dinner—but not at your house. I won't be hidden.' She stared at him.

'Oh? So what happened to private and intimate?' He shrugged. 'Very well, we shall dine at the Savoy.'

She gasped. 'I didn't mean that fancy.'

'You've said you want to dine there, so now is your chance.'

'I don't want your car picking me up. I'll take a taxi.' She stared at him. 'There and back.'

With her time at the library for ever over and tearful good-byes said, running eternally late, she dashed home to her little flat. There she hurriedly peeled off her skirt and blouse, then stood in the bath and used the overhead shower.

There was but one dress, and it was possibly too much even for such a luxury hotel—unless it was for a ball of course. But the restaurant…?

And yet she loved it.

And it was hers now.

The purple rental dress that she would keep for ever.

Maybe she'd end up doing the housework in it, but tonight it was calling to her.

'Come on,' she said, taking the gorgeous gown out of the wardrobe. 'We're going out. One last time.'

She dressed it down. Belted it and wore pretty flat sandals. Kept her hair loose.

She saw Sahir as she entered the restaurant, and he stood as she approached his table.

Her first instinct was to run to him—to somehow leap across the tables and rush to the man her heart desired.

Her second instinct was to run in the opposite direction. To flag down a taxi and race home. Because, yes, he made her feel strong—and yet somehow he weakened her too. She was terrified of capitulating…of agreeing to tonight, tomorrow, to a whole lifetime, even…

'Sahir.'

She took a seat and tried not to meet his eyes, yet she felt the seductive pull of him flood every pore. She saw a beau-tifully wrapped gift by her plate and recognised what it was. She tried to ignore it.

Even as his raised hand told the waiter to wait for a moment she recalled the heat of his palm on her skin, the touch of his fingers… And not just the intimate touches, but the way that hand had held her own.

She met his eyes. Today, so many things had ended. And while she might not have wanted them to…

'You haven't opened your gift.'

She would have liked to be strong enough to refuse it, but amongst all her regrets was one that she had no memento of their time together.

It was wrapped in silk and tied with gold cord, but she saw it was the book of poems and she held it to her face and inhaled it, shivering with delight.

'Thank you.' She put it on the table, but then changed her mind and put it in her bag, along with the silk and the cord. 'I don't want to spill anything on it.'

'Of course not.'

Violet put down the menu. 'Can I say something?'

She couldn't order and make it through a meal, just carry on eating, flirting, falling a little more under his spell.

She knew she was strong, but part of knowing your own strength was knowing your weakness—and Sahir would be hers for ever.

'I don't want to be your mistress.'

'Violet…'

'Please.' She put up her hand now, just as he had done as he told the waiter he did not want any interruptions. 'I knew you'd come. Maybe not today, but some day. But perhaps I'm being unjust. Maybe when you marry…'

She wanted him to be the man she wanted for herself.

The heat of the candle had her moving her hand, but he singed it with his fingers, and now she could touch him. She felt his lovely cheek and strong jaw.

'I don't steal.'

'Violet, please can we not—?'

'Please let me speak, Sahir.' She was finding it hard enough to articulate. 'I do have a compass, but not north and south… If I was your second wife, or whatever, it would be stealing. I believe a heart belongs to one person, and I couldn't do that to another woman. It would be taking something that wasn't mine, just because I want it, and it would hurt her. Anyway, I'm sick of being second best.'

He said nothing.

'I think I should go,' she said.

'Dine with me.'

'No.' Violet shook her head. 'Because then I'll forget all my own rules and we'll end up in bed. You know that. I know that…' She glanced over to where Layla and Maaz sat. 'They know that.'

'Okay,' he said. 'Can I speak now? Uninterrupted?'

'I won't stay.'

'You had your chance to speak,' he said.

She glanced over and waved to Maaz and Layla. 'Am I to be kidnapped again? Will they not let me leave?'

'You can leave any time. I just ask that you hear what I have to say. Although I would prefer us to have this conversation in private. I have a suite here…'

'I'm not falling for that. Like your massage.' She shook her head. She knew if she went to his suite they'd tumble into bed. And then she'd love him even more. And… 'No.'

'Why don't we just have dessert?'

She nodded, and stared at the menu, but then he spoke with the waiter and the gorgeous velvet folder was removed.

'I hadn't chosen.'

'Violet…' He sighed in exasperation. 'I'm trying to have a serious conversation.'

She'd hoped to sneak a copy of the menu, use it as a book-mark. But of course she couldn't tell him that, so she nod-ded, and stopped thinking about strawberry tarts and lemon meringues—oh, and chocolate and chestnut terrine.

'After that first night, when those images of us were briefly aired, my father saw them. He knew that his son was in love...'

She looked up.

'We barely knew each other then—' she attempted.

'Violet,' Sahir interrupted. 'We might not have realised it, but my father did. Aadil had alerted him to the threat, and then I called, requesting a week off.' He reached for her hand. 'I think by the end of that week perhaps we would have caught up with the same idea?'

She stared at his face, right into those eyes, and it was like watching a door open. It was as if she was being invited in— as if the noisy restaurant had disappeared and they were alone in the desert, or in a garden in London, or even her tiny flat.

It mattered not. They were in love...

'My father panicked...knew the danger. Because it is completely forbidden. A ruler can only...'

'I know the law.'

'My father...' He looked at her. 'He, more than most, knew the difficulties ahead if I broke that law.'

She wouldn't tell him what his father had shared with her, Sahir realised, and he was so proud of her for that.

Violet frowned as the waiter came over, carrying a silver tray. He removed the cloche and lit up the dessert so it danced with blue fire.

'I'll give it a miss,' she said, and gave him a smile.

'You don't want dessert?' asked Sahir.

'I don't like fruit cake, or pudding, or anything...' She went to grab her bag. 'I really must go.'

'Well, I asked the chef to prepare it especially. Apparently, it was my parents' favourite treat when they were in London...'

'Oh?' Violet said airily, as if she didn't already know.

'Now...' He took a jug and poured a very generous amount

of cream over the dessert, and then scooped up some brandy butter with a silver spoon and held it out.

She reached forward, took the spoon in her mouth—because at least a mouthful of pudding would stop her from being indiscreet.

Oh, dear.

She loathed brandy, but this tasted of rum—and she hated that even more. It was so thick and rich, and he was watching her chewing it, forcing it down, and then taking a drink of water…

'Here,' he said, taking another scoop, still watching as she grimaced for a second time. 'Violet, I know you and my father spoke.'

Thank goodness her mouth was full. She kept chewing.

'I know.' He nodded. 'My father was stunned that you hadn't told me.' He took her hand. 'I wasn't. I was proud. Violet, he panicked because he's unwell…'

He stopped. And as his eyes lifted Violet saw agony. She knew then just how serious this conversation was, especially with Layla and Maaz so close.

'Perhaps we could speak in private,' she said.

'Thank you.'

She was shaking as he led her out, and yet still she did not want to break the King's confidence, unsure just how much Sahir knew.

'We're not staying in the same suite they did…' he told her.

Her eyes widened. 'I'm not staying at all,' she corrected. 'We're just talking.'

'Of course.'

He opened a door, and the second it closed behind them she turned frantic eyes to him.

'The King is okay,' he said. 'Although last week they thought he needed surgery.'

'Where?'

'On his brain.'

She started to cry.

'Violet, it's going to be treated with radiation, and the tumour is very slow-growing. We pray he's going to be okay, but I couldn't come to you straight away.'

'Of course not.'

'I had to sort things out.'

'I know.'

'Come on.'

She walked into his suite and never before had she felt as if she was coming home. Here, in a hotel she'd never been to, for the first time in her life she felt as if she were home.

There were pale pink tulips in vases... And on the television screen there she was—standing on his balcony, her dress shimmering in the morning sun... And there was a trolley with the entire dessert menu laid out on it... And then she gasped, because on the mantelpiece there was a photo of her, with Sahir standing behind her, watching her.

'I've never been on someone's mantelpiece.'

There were little pieces of her everywhere.

'My favourite tea,' she said, and smiled, opening the jar.

'In case you decide to stay a little while.'

'I'm too needy to be a mistress. And I'm not just being moral—honestly, I'll be the most dreadful, demanding...'

'I only want you,' Sahir told her. 'You come first.'

Those words stopped her from speaking, from breathing. It was as if a terror she hadn't even known had left her.

'Hold out your hand.'

'Stop it.'

She wasn't sure this was happening—especially when he told her to place her palm up.

'Here...' He reached into his jacket pocket and pulled out not a ring, but a vial. In her palm she felt a cold sensation. Opening her eyes, she stared at the small heap of orange sand from his land.

'You pour it back into my palm,' Sahir said. 'If you want this to continue.'

'If I want *what* to continue?' Violet frowned.

Oh, what the hell?

She poured it into his palm and ground it in. And then she threw it away and kissed him, because those lips were irresistible.

'Violet…'

He moved to peel her back, but their time apart meant that was impossible, and he kissed her back so hard, so deeply, that she was sinking. And then she was being carried to a bed and kissed again. And it still felt like home because soon she was being made love to, her violet gown ruched around her waist and pulled down at the top, being kissed all over…

Being made love to by Sahir was what made it feel like home.

'You made me wait a week…' She smiled over to him.

'I had to source this.'

He reached over and opened a drawer. She saw a gorgeous polished wood box with a beautiful clasp.

'Purple diamonds are very rare.'

'Violet,' she corrected.

'Violet diamonds are even rarer.'

The ring was absolutely exquisite, almost in the shape of a heart, and he slipped it on her finger. But she was crying, and a little cross.

'You put me through hell for a week to get this? You could have called the library, or…'

He kissed her nose.

'It's complicated when a prince chooses his bride. I had to go to the desert for deep reflection—even though my decision was already made. Even though the council already approved.'

'The council approves?'

'They know I will not hide, and they know I will not take this lightly, so they agreed I could select the sand for our wedding.'

'I don't understand…'

'The sand you just threw…' He kissed her mouth. 'We have to find every grain.'

Her eyes widened.

'Will you marry me, Violet?' He put his hand up before she could answer. 'Before you say yes or no, know that if you accept then one day you will be Queen.'

'On one condition,' she said.

'It's a yes or no answer.'

'On one condition,' she said again, and stated her demand.

'That's never happened before.' He shook his head as she lay there silent. 'I can't see it working…'

'I can,' Violet said.

'Very well.' He nodded.

'Then I would love to be your wife.'

EPILOGUE

THE SERVICE WAS SIMPLE.

Marriage between a future king and his bride had always been a very low-key, matter-of-fact affair.

At least as far as the elders were concerned.

There were no bridesmaids, as such—well, not officially. But Grace helped Violet get into her gown.

'You look incredible…' Grace had tears in her eyes, watching love come alive.

'So do you,' Violet said, glancing at the tiny little bump that contained her niece or nephew, although not officially. 'I'm scared.'

'Of…?'

'Tripping over.'

'Not of marrying a prince and living overseas?'

'None of that,' Violet said. 'I just don't want to fall or…'

'You won't,' Grace said. 'And even if you do…'

Pria came to the door. It was time for Grace to take her place for the service.

She smiled at Violet. 'Whenever you are ready.'

'Thank you.'

It was very different from all the weddings she'd known before, because she could sit here alone for as long as she liked!

And actually Violet felt a little sick, with excited nerves—so, yes, she would make him wait, and make a little more dramatic entrance.

So she popped a mint, topped up her lip-gloss and let herself out of the Venus wing, having spent her last night there.

The palace was almost empty now, with most of the staff outside.

'Aadil.' She smiled at him.

'Violet,' he said, for the last time.

She'd be titled when they spoke next, and they were friends now. Each understood where the other was coming from.

'Your prince awaits,' he told her.

'Thank you,' she said as he opened the door to the King's private garden.

She made her way through the garden and there Sahir stood in a silver robe, beneath the tree where his parents had married, deeply in love, his mother pregnant with Sahir.

There were differences, though. For Sahir didn't hide his smile of delight when he saw his bride. In fact, they gazed at each other with that same look that had first got them into trouble.

Violet's heart felt as if it were full of sparklers, all fizzing as she walked towards him.

She wore a simple white dress with sliver slippers, and on her head she wore Queen Anousheh's favourite tiara, which the King had kindly offered for her to wear.

She wore her violet diamond engagement ring…and instead of flowers she carried a beautiful book that felt like a gift from above.

The King was smiling, and doing very well, seated with Ibrahim and Jasmine, who sat alongside Carter and Grace.

'You look beautiful,' Sahir told her. 'You always do.'

'Thank you.' She accepted his compliment. 'I did make quite an effort.' She looked at him, all trimmed and perfect, and she ached to kiss him, or pinch him—but of course did not. 'You did too.'

He nodded, and they turned to Hakaam.

Sahir poured some sand into her palm and Violet found out how she should have reacted the last time he'd done so.

Hakaam spoke. 'The sand always returns to the desert, but for now you share the wonders of the land.'

She carefully poured it back into Sahir's palm and it was carefully returned to two vials. Her palm was dusted, and so too was Sahir's, and both vials were sealed in golden wax by a very serious Hakaam as all the elders gathered round.

Violet closed her eyes when she thought of how she'd just brushed the sand to the floor and then kissed him.

Then Sahir gave her his promises.

'I accept,' Violet said.

She gave him her promises, and Sahir accepted them, adding that he would cherish them.

And, yes, there were more differences, and Hakaam had had to rework his charts. Because instead of being taken deep into the desert straight away, they were returning to the palace.

They stood outside the long doors and waited for them to be opened, and now Violet's one condition was to be met.

'This time, I *choose* to be photographed on the balcony,' she said.

They walked out to cheers, and photographers in helicopters, who captured the groom gazing at his wife, and the bride in a gown that was shot with silver catching the late-afternoon breeze.

And then it seemed Sahir could not resist, because he turned her around and she stared.

'You said no kissing.'

'Just a small one.'

It was scandalous, delicious and perfect, and she felt Sahir grip her hand.

Things would be different now.

And how the people cheered to see their grumpy king smiling. To see their crown prince with his gorgeous bride.

Love was no longer a secret, or something to fear in a ruler.

Today they all agreed that love made the world better.

* * *

At last they were flown into the desert, and the helicopter left them. But instead of heading to the tent, to attempt making the first of the many, many babies Violet wanted, Sahir stopped them.

'We have to check on the horses,' he said.

'On our wedding night?'

'No maids, no groomsmen—just us.'

'What's the point of being a princess?' she teased as they walked to the stables.

And there was Josie, squealing to be fed.

'If you want a pet, it comes with responsibility,' Sahir told her.

Then out she trotted, the gorgeous white foal, bounding towards her like an overgrown puppy, batting her lashes...

'She's *mine*?'

This time she embraced her without hesitation...absolutely.

Violet trusted in love.

* * * * *